Stocking Stuffer

A STEAMY CHRISTMAS ROMANCE

LAUREN SMITH

[signature]

Lauren
SMITH
TIMELESS ROMANCE

Edited by Noah Chinn

Cover art by Angela Haddon

The publisher is not responsible for websites (or their content) that are not owned by the publisher.

ISBN: 978-1-956227-55-0 (e-book edition)

ISBN: 978-1-956227-56-7 (print edition)

One

DECEMBER 23RD

"This costume does not fit." Bailey Willis plucked at the very short red velvet skirt trimmed with white fur that she wore and frowned. The candy-cane-style striped stockings came up to midthigh, leaving a few inches of bare thigh below her short skirt. The outfit looked cute, but it was way too sexy for her company's Christmas charity event.

"You look adorable," Cheryl gushed and handed her the red Santa hat.

"I thought I was supposed to be an elf." Bailey had been unlucky enough to be volunteered as an employee who would dress up for the costume part of the event. Cheryl, the head of Bailey's graphic design department at Trouble Inc., had put her up for the position, and Bailey couldn't say no. She'd only been working at Trouble Inc. for two months, and it was her dream job. The last thing she wanted to do was mess it up by not going along with stuff like this . . . even if it meant dressing up as a sexy Santa or an elf or whatever she was supposed to be. Not only that, but she was a bit worried she looked a little unprofessional for a company Christmas party.

"Is there going to be a Santa? Or is it just me?" Bailey tried to ignore how naked she felt in the costume. She was twenty-six years old, but she had never in all her life worn anything this revealing, except maybe a swimsuit, but this felt different. The red velvet top showed a few inches of her bare midriff, and it really didn't feel appropriate for work.

"There's going to be a Santa with you. He's some guy from floor twelve, one of the stuffy engineers."

"Great." Bailey tried to hide the sarcasm in her voice, but by Cheryl's chuckle she knew she had failed.

"It's only for a couple of hours. They wanted someone young and cute for the kids." Cheryl was in her forties and didn't seem to want to switch places with her.

"I guess I'm ready." Bailey straightened the little Santa hat on her head and stepped farther out of the bathroom stall where she'd just changed clothes. Thankfully, the resort hotel her company had booked for the Christmas party had a roomy bathroom near the ballroom.

"Everyone is going to love you." Cheryl played with Bailey's light brown hair, twisting her loose, wavy curls around a bit as though she were a Hollywood stylist.

2

"Let's go—the kids will be here soon." Cheryl opened the bathroom door and Bailey stepped out first.

Trouble Inc.'s company retreat was a yearly event. It was Bailey's first, of course, so she'd only heard stories secondhand about the lavish nature of the event the company's CEO insisted on paying for himself. He said it was a treat for his employees and a way of saying thank you for their hard work every year. Tonight would be a big fundraiser for a particular charity that was chosen each year by employee vote. This year they were supporting the Make-A-Wish Foundation. Twenty children and their families had been flown out to the resort, and they would receive prizes, including some presents that Bailey and whoever had gotten suckered into playing Santa would be handing out tonight.

"What am I supposed to do again?" Bailey whispered nervously as she and Cheryl headed toward the event hall doors, which were wide open.

Just beyond the doorway, there were a hundred large circular tables filled with people. The ceiling was glittering with crystal chandeliers which brightened the room like twinkling stars. A life-size Santa's village was set up just to the left of the stage that was big enough for Bailey to walk into.

"Just go into Santa's little cottage and wait until Santa and you are introduced. Then come out, wave, and be ready to greet the kids. They'll come and sit on Santa's lap,

3

and you can hand out presents after they talk with Santa. Each gift is assigned to a specific child, and the gifts are all grouped alphabetically."

Cheryl nudged Bailey in the direction of the village, and Bailey practically ran toward the shelter of the cute little cottage.

A few of the people at tables near her chuckled as she rushed past them to get into Santa's cottage.

Please let everyone drink enough wine tonight that they forget they saw me like this, she silently pleaded.

She reached the little cottage that had a "Santa's House" sign hanging above the doorway and twisted the knob. The interior of the cabin was surprisingly large, with a cozy living room complete with a fireplace, two armchairs, and a plate of cookies with a glass of milk laid on a nearby table. There was no sign of the Santa she'd been paired with so she stole a cookie and nibbled on it while she examined the rest of the cottage. Whoever had created this had thought of every little detail. A pair of fur-lined Nordic snow boots sat by the fireplace, and she bent over to pick one up. Behind her the cottage door opened.

"Now there's one hell of a nice Christmas gift," a deep, rumbling voice said with a chuckle from the doorway. It was a voice she knew almost better than her own, even if it was half an octave deeper than the last time she'd heard it.

She straightened and whirled around to see a tall man

dwarfing the entrance of the cottage. He had a Santa costume draped over his arm and a pair of black Santa boots in his other hand. Her eyes roved from his lean legs in a pair of blue jeans up to his gray T-shirt with some obscure grunge rock band logo on it. Then her eyes froze as they took in his face.

Montgomery Macholan. The boy she'd crushed on her entire childhood and teen years was standing right in front of her.

"Mack?" she gasped.

"Bailey?" He choked on her name, his eyes wide. "Holy fu—" He stopped himself and gave his head a little shake. His blonde hair was a little too long, and that toss of his head sent a lock of hair into his gray eyes.

God, Mack was still as hot as ever, infuriatingly so. He was even hotter than he'd been at eighteen, the last time she'd seen him before he left for college and broke her heart.

"What are you doing here, Mack?" she hissed and jerked him into the cottage. She shut the door, sealing them inside so no one at the tables nearby would overhear anything they were saying.

"Me? What are *you* doing here? Since when do you work at Trouble Inc.? Don't tell me—they hired you as some sort of sexy Santa elf, and you're really an exotic dancer now or something?"

For a second Bailey couldn't even blink. "Did you just

call me a stripper?" Her voice pitched up, and she was mortified at how much the man could upset her in less than thirty seconds.

"Well, you are dressed like one, and damn, Bailey, you grew up." His voice wasn't full of teasing, but rather he sounded impressed. No, he sounded in *awe* of her.

She glanced down, covered her skimpy top with her arms, and tried to curl in a little on herself to hide her exposed midriff.

"Put your eyes back in your head, Mack, and since when do you work here?"

He tossed the Santa suit on the armchair nearest him and frowned. It was the sexy kind of frown that made Bailey think of playing out a sexy Santa fantasy where she ended up getting spanked. And just like that, she was hot and bothered, all thanks to freaking Montgomery Macholan. How could one man she hadn't seen in ten years make her feel like a lovestruck teenage girl all over again, albeit this time with more adult fantasies?

"I've been working here since college. I'm in the engineering division," he explained.

"You're the one they sent from the engineering side?" She groaned a little too loudly. The Santa suit he carried was a dead giveaway, but she hadn't wanted to accept it. Now they were stuck playing a game of North Pole house for the next hour.

"Hey, I didn't volunteer. I lost a bet with some of the

guys, and—" He halted as sudden applause filled the ball-room. "Shit, that's the boss on stage. I need to change now." He glanced through the frosted windows of the cottage and reached for the fly of his jeans.

"Mack, you can't just—"

But it was too late—he shoved his jeans down, showing off a tight ass covered in black briefs and muscled legs as he kicked off his shoes. Then he pulled the Santa suit pants on and cinched the drawstring tight at the waist. After that, he put the heavy Santa coat on over his t-shirt and buttoned it up. There was no heavy fake belly for him to wear, but the padded coat gave an appearance of a bulkier Santa body. Bailey just stared as he sank his sock-clad feet into the shiny black boots. Finally, when she remembered what the hell they were supposed to be doing, she shoved his Santa hat and beard at him as he finished buttoning the coat.

They both peered through the windows, listening to Maxwell Andrews, the CEO, as he spoke about the company's chosen charity, the Make-A-Wish Foundation. There was another round of applause as he announced the arrival of the children.

"We have a special guest for them tonight. Santa and one of his elves came a very long way from the North Pole to give them some presents. Kids, are you ready?" Maxwell's booming voice asked, and little voices from the crowd cheered.

"Santa, come on out here!" Maxwell called over the microphone.

"That's our cue, I guess," Mack said. "Do I look okay?" he asked as he faced Bailey. His beard was too low below his chin.

"You need to fix just one thing," Bailey purred and waved a finger for him to come closer.

With a devilish grin, Mack leaned in toward her. She pulled the edge of his beard away from his face and pretended like she was going to kiss him. His gaze lowered to her lips, and with a wicked smirk she released the elastic beard from her hand and let it snap back on his face with a loud *thwack!*

"Ow!" he snapped. "I'm going to—" His growl was cut off as she opened the door behind him and, with a hard shove, pushed him out ahead of her. He halted awkwardly for a second before he slipped into his role as Santa Claus. A dozen children crossed the ballroom floor toward Mack and Bailey, their little faces bright with excitement, and that was when the snow began to fall.

Mack glanced up as the first few flakes tickled his nose. A fake snow machine high above their heads near the event lighting was unleashing a decent snowfall around the village. The children gasped, and the crowd of adults whispered excitedly. Even Mack was impressed. Maxwell Andrews really went all out for the kids this year. It actually looked like a part of the North Pole had been transported here by some kind of magic.

A smile curved Mack's lips. When he'd lost a bet with the guys in his department, he had thought this wasn't going to be fun. Now that he was here, seeing the snow and the faces of the kids who had been through medical hell on their own, he was damn proud to play Santa for them.

He shot a glance at the sexy elf who had joined him outside the cottage.

Bailey Willis.

Damn, she was just as gorgeous as she had been ten years ago. They had known each other their entire lives. Their houses had been next door to each other on the same little street, and their bedroom windows had faced each other. He was two years older than Bailey, but she'd always tagged along after him and his friends. It had been annoying, then cute, and finally dangerous.

That last spring before he'd left for college, he had been eighteen and the things he'd dreamed about doing to her . . . Well, they hadn't been PG. She'd been sixteen and he had done the smart thing. He'd gotten the hell out of there before he did something stupid. He would be lying if he said he hadn't thought of her in the last ten years. He had, *a lot*. Maybe too much. But he had stayed disciplined and not looked her up on social media, no matter how tempted he had been. Somehow, the thought of looking her up, seeing her dating or married, didn't seem like a good idea. His mom had mentioned a few times when Bailey had a boyfriend, and he'd shut down the conversation fast.

He knew she didn't want to see him ever again, and he was afraid that if he saw her, he'd make an ass of himself. Which was exactly what was happening right now. He was living out some sexy elf or Mrs. Claus fantasy with her at this very moment. He had to keep focused on the kids and not on the very questionable outfit someone had picked for Bailey to wear. Those candy-striped stockings covering most of her gorgeous legs and the cute red heels were not helping.

"Do you know what we' re supposed to do?" he whispered to Bailey.

"Uh-huh. The kids have assigned presents. You have each kid tell you their name, and I'll find their gift so you can give it to them."

"Got it." He adjusted the white beard and mustache. The thing itched, but it wasn't too annoying.

He headed for the red velvet armchair and sat down as the twenty or so kids lined up in front of him. He waved the first kid forward, and a shy girl with a fuzzy knit cap on her head came toward him. She perched on his knee and smiled.

"What's your name?" he asked.

"Liza Gutez," she replied. Her big brown eyes melted Mack's heart. Even though her face was too pale, she was still bright-eyed with joy.

"What have you always wanted for Christmas?" he asked, wondering what Maxwell had selected for her present.

Liza seemed to take this question very seriously. "To spend Christmas at home and not at the hospital."

Fuck. Mack swallowed hard. That wasn't something he could give her. Bailey made a soft little sound of distress behind him. He didn't dare look at her. She was such a softy, and if he saw tears in her eyes, he wouldn't stand a chance.

"Does your family spend Christmas with you at the hospital?"

Liza nodded. "They do."

"Then you know what?" Mack asked, somehow managing to find a smile, even though little Liza was breaking his damn heart.

"What?" she asked in a conspiratorial whisper, as though convinced he was about to share some North Pole secret with her.

"*Home* isn't a place—it's the *people* who love you. No matter where you are, Christmas is always with you because your home is where your heart is." He pointed a leather-gloved finger at the girl's chest, and she smiled broadly.

"Now, I believe we have a present for you." He turned to Bailey and couldn't miss her sniffle as she hastily dug through the pile of presents. She came back with a red envelope and handed it to Mack. He held it out to Liza, who opened the thick red paper. She stared at the sheet and frowned.

"What does it say?" she asked. Mack held it up a little so he could read it to her.

"It says you and your family have three weeks of private nurses to help you celebrate Christmas at your house instead of at the hospital." As soon as he finished reading this, he shot a glance at Maxwell, who was no longer on stage but instead speaking with a set of parents that he guessed were Liza's by the stunned looks on their faces. Private nurses weren't cheap. Maxwell had given the girl exactly what she wanted. The man was a wizard.

"Thank you, Santa!" Liza threw her arms around Mack's neck, and he embraced the child carefully. She was so small and frail.

"Just remember, Liza, you are strong, and nothing can stop you," he whispered in her ear and gave her an extra squeeze.

She scampered off toward her parents, clutching the envelope like it was the key to a magical kingdom built just for her.

The next several children were all just as sweet as Liza. Mack lost himself in the role of Santa Claus, throwing out *Ho ho ho*s and telling the children all about his flying reindeer and the elves working hard on toys for children all around the world. Bailey helped match the gifts with each child. By the time they finished, Maxwell was back on stage, a microphone in his hand.

"Let's thank Santa and his elf for bringing such magic to this room tonight. Let's give them a round of applause."

The adults at the banquet tables clapped loudly, and the children joined their families at their tables while dinner was brought out to the attendees.

"How about we create some magic of our own," Maxwell said, and he began describing through the silent auction items and helping increase the bids by offering donation matches.

"I think we can get changed now," Bailey whispered and jerked her head toward the cottage. The second the cottage door closed and they were certain no one would hear them, Mack crossed his arms and blocked the path to freedom with his body.

"So, little Bailey Willis works at Trouble Inc. How on earth did I not know that?"

Bailey shuffled nervously in her sexy red heels. Fuck, she was so adorable. He wanted to peel those striped stockings down her legs and push that fur-lined skirt up and—

"There are more than seven hundred employees in a ten-story building. It's honestly amazing we even met like this. We could have gone another decade without seeing each other if it hadn't been for this Santa stuff." She waved about the cottage with one hand.

"I would have noticed you anywhere," Mack said in a soft voice as he lowered his arms. "How long have you been working here?"

"A few months. I'm in graphic design." Bailey kept her answers short, and Mack knew she didn't want to talk to him. He wouldn't have either if he were her. That's what happened when you broke someone's heart when they were sixteen.

"Graphic design? I didn't know you were into that."

"There are a lot of things I'm into that you don't know about." Her eyes tracked up and down his body, and he couldn't help but wonder if any of those things she mentioned involved him.

Was it possible she still felt something for him? Or was it just two adults who had a desire for each other on a physical level but nothing more? Mack knew he should keep his damn mouth shut, but something about Bailey always made him do the stupidest things.

He removed the Santa coat and slipped out of the boots. He paused when he reached for the drawstring on the red velvet Santa pants. Bailey's eyes were glued to his crotch, and he had to fight hard not to react the way any hot-blooded man would when a gorgeous woman was looking at his groin.

"You like what you see, elf?" He slowly pulled the drawstring, loosening the pants. Bailey's stare snapped upward, and she covered her eyes with one hand as he dropped his Santa pants to the floor. It was way too much fun messing with her. It reminded him of the good old days before the night of his senior prom, when he'd fucked everything up.

"Put on some damn pants, Mack," Bailey growled, and it made him think of a puppy baring its teeth. He wanted to cuddle her. Which he shouldn't do . . . because he was the bastard who had broken her heart.

Bailey bent, her hand still covering her eyes as she tossed his jeans at him. The second he caught them, she made her escape out the door. By the time he'd emerged from the back door to Santa's cottage, he was wearing his own clothes again, and there was no sign of the sexy little elf in the crowded ballroom. Bailey Willis had escaped.

Two

"Where the hell are my clothes?" Bailey stood in the resort bathroom just outside the ballroom where she had changed earlier. There were no signs of her jeans, sweater, or boots.

She shivered and rubbed her bare arms as goosebumps broke out on her skin. Had Cheryl taken her clothes? She could go back in the ballroom, but Mack was there. She didn't want to see him. How unfair was it that guys could be so cute in high school, and then ten years later they were hot enough to melt the panties off every woman in a half-mile radius by simply breathing? Not only that, but it was clear he was even more of a flirt than ever.

When they were kids, he had always teased her. He used to mess up her hair in the hallway when he knew she spent an hour each morning trying to tame it before school. Then he would come along and rough it up with his hand, and *oooh*, she had hated that so much. Now . . . now she looked back on that and saw it for what it was. A boy tugging on a girl's pigtails. He'd liked her, she had known that then, but she'd also known he hadn't liked her *enough*. He always defaulted to a big-brother role like he had the night of his senior prom when she'd only been a sophomore. But Bailey wasn't going to let herself think about that night. Never again.

With a little growl of frustration, she pulled out her cell phone from the tiny pocket in her red velvet miniskirt. She sent a text to Cheryl's phone, asking where her clothes were. She waited . . . and *waited*. No text came back. It was like a bad prank, but she knew Cheryl hadn't done this on purpose. Most likely she was in the ballroom socializing with the other employees. Maybe Bailey could sneak back up to her hotel room and change into some other clothes while she waited for Cheryl to check her phone.

With that plan in mind, Bailey exited the resort bathroom and slipped down the hall toward the bay of elevators that would take her to the hotel rooms. She tapped one red heel impatiently and did her best to ignore the smirks of a few men in the hotel bar across from the elevators.

"Hey, Santa baby, come and sit on my lap. I'll tell you what I want for Christmas," one of the men jeered. The others with him all hooted with laughter. Their faces were splotched with red, and Bailey could smell the alcohol from where she stood ten feet away.

"Don't upset her," one chortled. "She might put coal in your stocking."

"I wouldn't care, if I got her on her back. Imagine those candy cane legs thrown over my shoulders."

Okay, that was enough. Bailey wasn't naturally confrontational. She had a live-and-let-live approach to life, but these guys? She was ready to shove coal where the sun didn't shine. She slowly removed the little Santa hat from her head and started to turn around.

The jeering and inappropriate remarks grew as the men stupidly assumed that she was going to respond positively to such sexist comments.

"My lap's all warm for you." One man slapped his thigh, and Bailey saw red. She'd always thought that was just a dramatic turn of phrase, but an actual cloud of red filled her vision. She stomped toward them, but someone grabbed her arm and spun her wildly away from the men in the bar. She smacked into a hard, warm body.

"Hey, honey, thanks for waiting for me. Ready to go up to our room?" Mack wrapped his arms around her lower back and grinned down at her like a man wildly in love. For a second, she had no idea what was going on— she just stared up at him, completely entranced by the look in his eye and the way his voice was so soft, sexy, and deep. Her skin tightened, and she basked in the warmth of his body against hers. She was in Mack's arms. It felt so incredible, and yet she didn't understand why he was acting like this.

"I . . ."

He leaned his head down to hers, nuzzling her nose, his lips feathering hers as he whispered, "Play along—they're watching."

Play along . . . Of course. He didn't actually love her. He was taking the heat off her from those drunken jerks. Relief and disappointment battled within her, and her head dropped a slight inch away from his.

His hold on her tightened, and he jerked her attention back up to his face and the heat blazing there. Even if it was pretend, it felt real.

Well, screw it. If they were playing this game, she'd get that kiss she'd always wanted from him.

"Thanks, honey," she purred and stood up on her tiptoes, kissing him.

His arms around her tensed for a second before he dove into the act with her. He pulled her even closer, caging her completely in his hold. His lips gently forced hers open so he could thrust his tongue into her mouth in the most decadent, sinful way possible. She'd dated a decent number of men in the last ten years, and none of them had kissed her like this. Mack's tongue was making love to her mouth in thrusting patterns that mimicked what his body would do.

Heat exploded between her thighs, and she whimpered as he dug his fingers into her back in a sinful punishment, like a possessive wolf taming its mate. That image made her throb with a sensual need so violent that it stunned her. All she could think about was how it would feel for Mack to fuck her hard like a wild animal. *Oh God* . . . She tried to jerk away, but he kept her against him. She gasped for breath as he let their mouths part softly.

His lips feathered from her jaw to her ear before he bit her earlobe. Then he murmured in her ear, "That'll teach the pricks." He stepped back and shot a smirk at the men behind her.

"Let's go upstairs." He took her hand and led her into the elevator just as the doors opened. She followed, her body still flushed all over and her ears ringing from that kiss. It was like a lust bomb had been detonated in her head and no rational thoughts could penetrate the cloud of desire. So that's what kissing a grown-up Mack felt like.

The elevator doors closed, leaving them alone, and her sanity rushed back, leaving her a little light-headed from the swift change.

"Why did you do that? I could have handled those assholes." She hadn't needed Mack to sweep in and rescue her, and she definitely hadn't wanted it either.

He leaned against the back of the elevator and crossed his arms over his chest. It called attention to the muscles of his bare forearms. A flash of memory permeated her mind, a seventeen-year-old Mack leaning against his car door as she watched on her porch. Back then he'd looked irresistible. Now it was ten times worse. He was grown, his muscles were bigger, and the way he held himself spoke of the confidence of a man.

"I know you could've handled them," he chuckled, the soft, sexy sound rumbling out of him. "You would have handled them so well, in fact, that they would all have ended up in hospital beds."

She frowned. She wasn't violent, really, but she didn't let men be sexist jerks either.

"I remember when you kicked Dean Farris in the crotch after he made fun of your boobs on the first day of school when you were eight," he added. "Dean couldn't walk for a whole week. I can only imagine what a grown-up Bailey could do."

Mortification turned Bailey's face hot. "I didn't even have boobs back then. That's why I got so mad when he said that."

"Yeah, well, he was an idiot," Mack acknowledged.

"He was." She laughed a little at the memory. "He was actually a lot nicer to me when we got to high school." She hadn't minded Dean so much then. He never made fun of her again, and he was quiet.

"No man ever insults a woman who knees him with a nut shot. Trust me. He probably remembered that pain every time you looked at him," Mack said with far too much glee.

"It's not funny," Bailey growled. "I got sent to the principal's office, and you laughed at me."

That was something she wouldn't forget either. Mack had passed by the main office while he was running an errand for his fourth grade teacher, and he had seen her sitting on the dreaded wooden bench outside the principal's office. He had walked over and asked, *"What did you do wrong, champ?"* and patted her on the head. She had smacked his hand away, and he had walked off laughing... just like he was laughing now.

Boy, nothing ever really changed?

The elevator door chimed for her floor, and she stomped past him toward her room. He followed on her heels as she paused in front of her room and searched the flimsy elf costume for her room key . . . and came up empty-handed.

No key. No clothes. God, she was so screwed.

She growled and kicked her hotel door with one red shoe.

"Problem?" Mack asked.

She pressed her forehead to the door and sighed. "Just go away, Mack. Let me wallow in peace."

"Why didn't you change your clothes?" he asked.

"Because Cheryl took my clothes, and I can't get a hold of her."

"Now you can't get into your room to get your other clothes," he surmised.

"Wow, you're on a roll today." She didn't normally like to be sarcastic, but her mood had soured since she couldn't get away from him.

"Look, why don't you stay in my room, and I'll go find this Cheryl person?"

"Mack—"

"Bailey Willis, I'm older and wiser, and you better do what I say." He fixed her with a mock glare that brought back a hundred memories of being a little girl and hearing him say that.

She reacted purely out of habit and stuck her tongue out at him the way she had as a kid. A blaze of dangerous fire lit his gray eyes until they were fascinatingly mercurial, and she couldn't look away. For a long second neither of them moved. Then he blinked, severing the spell he had cast on her. He walked a few feet down the hall to the room next to hers and used a key card to open the door.

"You're seriously in the room next door?" Bailey groaned. The universe had clearly taped a Kick Me sign to her back.

He pushed his door wide open and waved for her to go inside.

"Wait here. I'll find Cheryl. What's her last name?"

"Morton."

"Right. Cheryl Morton from the graphic design

department." He paused at the door, one hand braced, keeping it open as he looked at her. "Don't go anywhere, okay?"

The hint of something she couldn't quite identify in his tone made her banish all thoughts of sneaking out of the room once he was gone. Mack could still read her mind, even after ten years apart.

"Yes, sir," she replied cheekily, hoping to defuse the girlish hope that his tone created inside her.

"Smart-ass." He chuckled and left her alone in his hotel room.

She waited a full minute before she gave in to her desire to snoop. He had brought a small weekender bag with him, probably planning to spend one night here as did she. Not everyone was staying at the hotel tonight. She knew some employees had opted to do so, but those with families would likely head home.

Bailey was staying just one night before she left. This would be the first time in two years she would be home for Christmas. She and Mack had, without talking to each other since that night at prom, somehow fallen into a schedule of returning home for Christmas on the opposite years so they never had to see each other. It made Bailey wonder where Mack would go this year, since it was his year to stay away. She had heard from her mother that he often went to tropical beaches or faraway places on the years that he didn't come home. It always left a hollow ache in her chest to think of Mack on a sunny beach, sipping a cocktail and kissing some buxom beach bunny every year.

Bailey trailed her fingertips over the buttery-smooth leather of his bag before she peeked inside. One of his dress shirts was on top, and she touched the light blue fabric. Feeling completely ridiculous, she lifted it to her face and breathed in his scent, which clung to the clothing. She closed her eyes, and the past blindsided her.

Ten years ago

The ballroom was packed with people gyrating excitedly to the music. Colored lights swept over the room in dizzying patterns. Bailey grinned as her date, Ty Evans, led her to the dance floor. She was just a sophomore, but one of the hottest senior football players had asked her to prom. Sophomores had to be asked by a junior or senior, and they had to get a permission slip signed by their parents. Thankfully, her parents hadn't seen a problem with it. Mack would be there, of course, to watch over her. He had decided to go with some of his friends from the tennis team, but he'd promised her parents he would keep an eye on her. It was *so* embarrassing, but at least she got to go to prom, while most of her friends couldn't.

Ty pulled Bailey close, his hands gripping her hips as

they started to dance. The music was fast, and Bailey tried to move, but Ty kept grinding against her. It wasn't that fun or comfortable, but she tried to enjoy it. After a few songs, she saw Mack a dozen feet away with one of the seniors, a gorgeous brunette named Allison, a girl Bailey knew from French club. Allison was nice, and Bailey liked her. Allison and Mack were laughing and spinning around, dancing the way that Bailey wanted to dance.

"Ty!" She tried to shout her partner's name over the loud music pumping out of the speakers around the room.

"Yeah?" he hollered back.

"Can we dance like that?" She pointed at Mack and Allison.

Ty followed her finger and frowned. "Aw, come on, Bailey. That's no fun. You're so hot, and this is so much better." He pulled her tighter to him, and Bailey sighed. This really sucked. She'd thought coming here tonight would be fun, that somehow Mack would see her, maybe ask her to dance when Ty went off to hang with his friends. She hadn't thought Ty would stick to her like glue and try to dry hump her all night.

"Can we get a drink?" she asked him.

He rolled his eyes but led her off the dance floor. When she cast one glance back at Mack, he was still dancing with Allison, but his eyes caught and held hers for a brief second, a clear question in his gaze as if to ask if she was okay. She gave him a tiny nod, and he focused back on his dance partner.

Ty stopped at one of the tables and grabbed two cups of red punch. Then they headed to the edge of the dance floor. He opened his black tuxedo jacket and pulled out a small flask and dumped part of its contents in his cup.

"Want some?" He held out the flask.

"No, I don't—" she started, but when she saw Mack lean down and kiss Allison, Bailey's chest crushed in on itself, her ribs stabbing her heart and obliterating it.

"Yeah, give me some." She grabbed the flask and poured some into her punch cup and downed the entire cup in a few deep gulps.

"Now that's what I'm talking about," Ty laughed and wrapped an arm around her waist. "Let's get out of here. Dancing is boring as fuck anyways."

They left the dance hall and headed into the parking lot. Ty had picked her up in his Range Rover, which she'd thought was fun. But now she was all too aware of how big the back seat was, especially when she and Ty sat in it together.

"So, Bailey, how are you enjoying your first prom?" Ty asked as he pulled a second flask out from underneath the driver's seat of the car. Where had he gotten all these flasks?

"It's been fun," she lied. This was the farthest thing

from fun she could think of. Seeing Mack and Allison kissing . . . a wave of nausea rolled over her.

"Here, have a little more," Ty suggested and offered her the second flask.

"No thanks." Bailey was starting to regret the alcohol she'd had in her punch.

"Suit yourself." Ty lounged back on his side of the seat and casually stretched an arm behind her shoulders. After a moment, he let it drop to touch her.

"You don't have to sit so far away," he said with a laugh and pulled her closer.

Bailey let him move her a little closer to him, but her mind was racing as she tried not to think of Mack and why seeing him with Allison literally felt like it was killing her.

"Um, Ty, could you take me home?" she asked in a small voice. "I don't feel so good, and—"

"Come on, Bailey," he crooned. "Tonight was supposed to be fun, and you are not being fun." He lifted her chin so she had to face him. "I know you have the hots for Macholan, but he doesn't date down. I do, though, and you bagged yourself a hot quarterback, babe, so enjoy it."

Before Bailey could react, his mouth was on hers, kissing her. His lips were hot and a little wet and suffocating. He pushed her almost roughly onto her back on the seat and came down on top of her.

The alcohol slowed Bailey's reactions just enough that she couldn't stop him from pinning her down.

"Ty, *get off*," she demanded in frustration as she jerked her face away from his. He only moved his mouth to her neck.

"Don't be a buzzkill, Bailey. You're a fucking sophomore. If you want to come to the prom with a senior, you gotta give me what I want."

"What do you want?" Bailey snapped and thrashed beneath him. He was too strong, though. She hadn't realized that until she couldn't get him off her.

"Stop being a baby—" Ty didn't get a chance to finish. The car door behind him opened, and suddenly he was ripped off Bailey and hit the ground with a thud.

"What the fuck—Macholan, you piece of shit!" Ty surged to his feet, and Bailey shoved her dress down her legs just in time to see Mack duck as Ty swung a fist.

Mack had come to save her. The thought rang inside her head like church bells, making her giddy. The alcohol didn't help the feeling, and she winced and closed her eyes as the world tilted and spun. The sounds of fighting just feet away made her eyes fly open again, though. Mack punched Ty hard in the face, and Ty went down, landing in a lump on the asphalt.

"Mack?" Bailey crawled to the edge of the back seat and stared at him. He was breathing hard, and his lip was split. A tiny trickle of blood dripped down his chin. He wiped it away with the back of his hand and glanced at her.

"You okay?" he asked. His voice was gruff.

Bailey answered with a nod.

"Good. Get your purse. I'm taking you home."

"But, Mack—"

"You're going home, Bailey," he barked in a tone that hurt her much more than a physical blow ever could.

She grabbed her small black clutch purse from the floor and scrambled out of the car. Mack was already striding away toward his car, and Bailey ran after him.

"Get in." He opened the passenger door for her, and she fell into the seat. As much as she wanted to go back to the dance with Mack, she was definitely feeling tired, thanks to the alcohol. Mack climbed in the driver's seat and gunned the engine.

They didn't speak the entire time he drove her home. When he parked the car in her driveway, he turned the engine off and stared straight ahead. A tic worked in his jaw, and he finally looked at her.

"What the hell were you thinking?" He didn't shout, didn't even growl this. His question was a whisper, which sliced her deep.

"I wasn't," she said hoarsely. "I just . . ." She didn't dare say that she'd left with Ty because seeing Mack dance with and kiss someone else had obliterated her.

"You are smarter than this, Bailey. Never drink with a

guy you don't trust with your life. And don't drink until you're twenty-one."

"You're not my father or my brother, Mack," she said softly, but there was a bite to her tone she couldn't hold back. "You can't boss me around."

"No, I'm definitely not your brother or father," he muttered. "Why don't you date a nice sophomore, some kid who looks at you with stars in his eyes like you deserve? Not some asshole like Ty."

"I don't want that." She turned away, her hand touching the car door. He reached across her, his hand covering hers.

"What do you want?" he asked.

The tension in the car was suffused with electricity, and as Bailey lifted her tear-filled eyes to his, she blurted out the truth.

"I want you."

Mack let out a soft exhale, his eyes closing as Bailey's heart leapt. This was it—he was going to kiss her. She closed her eyes and waited for the most magical moment of her life to happen. Her first kiss with Mack. His warm breath fanned her face; he smelled of mint, and that only excited her more. But the kiss never came, at least not on her lips. Mack instead pressed his mouth to her forehead.

"Go on to bed, Bailey. Take two Tylenol and drink a bottle of water before you go to sleep so you won't have a headache in the morning."

Bailey opened her eyes as he pulled away. She was numb. *So numb.* She barely remembered exiting the car or walking up to her front door.

Don't look back, please don't look back, she begged herself.

She didn't.

Bailey let go of the memories of the past, pushing them away in her mind, but they always seemed to drift back in on her when she least expected it. She dropped Mack's shirt back into his bag and stomped away from the bed. *Mack's bed.*

God . . . for the last ten years, she had managed not to see him even once after he'd graduated. Yet everything she'd felt for him came flooding back with one little breath of his scent.

"I'm an addict. I'm addicted to him. He's like a drug," she moaned and covered her face with her hands.

She needed to get her clothes and get out of here. Maybe she wouldn't stay the night after all. She could pay the cancellation fee and go home a day early. Yeah, that's what she'd do. If she stayed one night *and one room* away from Mack she'd never get to sleep.

Three

Mack got off the elevator and noticed that the three men in the bar who had been harassing Bailey were still there. They were drinking and roaring with laughter. Mack paused, his hands curled into fists as he let himself imagine what he would do to them if he ever saw them in a dark alley with no witnesses.

Just cool it. They are men with tiny dicks who aren't worth going to jail over.

He released a breath and walked past the bar and headed for the new resort ballroom. He searched the crowd of Trouble Inc. employees. Mack had no idea what Cheryl looked like.

"Hey, Macholan, nice job!" someone called out as he walked past. He turned his head to see his department head, a guy in his midfifties named Riggs. Riggs had been the source of the bet for how he ended up as Santa Claus.

Mack gave him a mock salute. The guy was like a favorite uncle to him, a real lovable but tough boss. He had been a mentor to Mack since the first day Mack had started working at Trouble Inc. Mack scanned the people nearest him and then pulled out his cell phone. He logged into the employees' area of the company's website and scrolled down to the graphic design department. He saw a picture of Cheryl. Memorizing her face, he went back to examining the crowd. He found her about twenty feet away, talking to several people at one of the tables. She laughed at something someone said. He grinned; she was a social butterfly, and he bet she got along well with Bailey.

He remembered Bailey could be a little shy at first, but when she was around other friendly people she blossomed into a confident person. There was so much he'd thought he knew about her, but now, after a ten-year absence, he was realizing there was much he didn't know. Like graphic design. When had she gotten into art? He remembered she used to doodle sometimes, but it hadn't seemed like anything serious. How much had he missed about her in high school and college? Apparently, a lot.

He couldn't get the image of Bailey up in his hotel room and how she looked in the elf costume out of his head. God, it was a temptation no man could resist. But she hated him . . . because he had done the right thing as a kid and walked away from her. It wasn't as though Mack could walk up to her and explain, "Hey, sorry I didn't kiss you that night, because I would've wanted to do more, and if we did more it would have been illegal since I was eighteen and you weren't." Yeah, she wouldn't care. She would only remember that moment he'd pulled away.

He couldn't tell her how he'd felt watching her walk into the dance hall on Ty's arm. Seeing that moronic meathead touching her, grinding on her like some fool . . . Mack had done his best to have a good time with his own friends, and when Allison had asked him to dance, he'd agreed. She was the one who'd kissed him, but he would admit he went along with it, if only to get his mind off Bailey and that quarterback. When they left the dance, he had to go after them. He knew what Ty was like and that he might try something. Bailey was tough, but Ty could overpower her, and Mack had to protect her.

He was afraid he was too late when he had seen the fogged-up windows of Ty's SUV. When he'd pulled the asshole off her, she was okay. Scared, but okay. He had been furious—not at her, but at himself. He never should have told her parents it was safe for her to go with Ty. All because he had secretly thought he might get one dance with the cute girl next door before he left for college.

He had never gotten that dance. Instead, he had broken her heart.

Mack squared his shoulders and pushed his way through the throng of people until he reached Cheryl.

"Cheryl?" he cut in when there was a lull in the woman's conversation.

"Yes?" She faced him, brows raised.

"Bailey Willis needs her street clothes. She thought you might know where they are."

"Oh my God!" Cheryl gasped. "Yes, I completely forgot. I bet she wants to kill me." Cheryl excused herself from the other people at the table and waved for Mack to follow her.

She stopped at another table and held up a shopping bag. "Her clothes are inside. Do you want me to take them to her?"

"No, it's fine. I'll take them," Mack assured her and accepted the bag she held out.

He was almost out the ballroom when a voice stopped him.

"Montgomery."

He spun to see Maxwell Andrews smiling at him.

"Mr. Andrews." He nodded respectfully. Andrews was a few years older than him and one hell of a boss, so Mack always treated him with the greatest respect.

"You make a great Saint Nick. The kids loved it. It meant a lot to their parents."

Mack's throat tightened at the unexpected praise. "Thank you, sir."

"I know you did it because you lost a bet to Riggs, but you did make an incredible Santa. I just wanted you to know." Andrews grinned and turned and walked away.

How the hell did Andrews know about the bet? It wasn't exactly something he and Riggs had shouted from the rooftops. It was just the usual departmental competition crap.

He was a wizard, that's what Andrews was.

Mack smiled and returned to the elevator bay, but as he passed by the bar and restaurant his stomach grumbled. He and Bailey had missed the event dinner. A place like this resort would have excellent room service. He walked over to the bar to flag down a bartender.

"Could I get a room service menu, please?"

"Sure." The man handed Mack a folded menu.

"Thanks." Mack stepped back toward the elevators, humming softly to himself. Bailey was in his room. His hotel room. That shouldn't have made him so happy, but it did. He had a moment to talk to her again, to *see* her again. He was suddenly seeing everything in a new light.

She wasn't sixteen anymore. He wasn't eighteen. They were both adults, for God's sake. Maybe . . . maybe he could finally have that sweet kiss she had offered him ten years ago. He hadn't planned on their first kiss being in front of those assholes in the bar. There was only one problem. Bailey clearly hadn't forgiven him for rejecting her on prom night. That meant he had to remind her that she used to like him. He touched his lips as he replayed that scorching make-out scene they'd had in front of those drunk assholes. He had told Bailey they were pretending. But nothing about that had been faked. She had sent him skyrocketing off into space with just her mouth.

Mack chuckled. He knew what she would say if she were privy to his thoughts.

"You can't handle me, Mack," she would say. She might be right. Little Bailey Willis wasn't just a firecracker. She was goddamn dynamite, and she would completely blow him away.

If he could only convince her . . .

Maybe he just needed to seduce her the old-fashioned way, Mack style. Starting with room service. He chuckled as he stepped off the elevator.

Bailey sat up at the sound of the door opening, and her shoulders sagged in relief as she saw the bag Mack carried.

"Are those my clothes?"

"Yep. I found Cheryl. She was chatting away and forgot. She's very sorry, by the way." Mack presented the clothes to her with a flourish.

She practically snatched the bag away from him and bolted for the bathroom rather than the door. She really didn't want to be standing in the hallway trying to find her room key if another drunk jerk came down the hall.

"At the risk of you kicking my ass, I must say, I'm going to miss those striped stockings." His teasing chuckle made her pose in the bathroom doorway, her heart giving a traitorous flutter.

She had the sudden desire to drive him crazy for her. It would serve him right to get him all worked up and then leave. Normally, she would have thought that it was a bitchy thing to do, but he completely deserved it.

"Oh yeah?" She looked at him over her shoulder and dropped her clothing bag on the bathroom counter.

Mack was sitting on the side of the bed facing her, leaning back on his forearms, seemingly utterly relaxed. His T-shirt was pulled tight over his chest, accenting his muscles.

Focus, Bailey. This is about torturing him, not letting him torture you.

She bent and stepped out of her red heels and lifted the fur-lined edge of her skirt just enough to show off the rest of her bare thigh as she started rolling one stocking down her leg.

The bed creaked softly, and she knew he had moved. She smirked as she peeled the stocking off and tossed it in his direction. He caught it with one hand, and she removed her second stocking, swinging it playfully before tossing it at him as well. He caught the second one and bolted off the bed, moving purposely toward her, a predatory heat in his eyes. She retreated at the last second and slammed the bathroom door in his face.

"What the fuck, Bailey," he growled from the other side of the door.

Half of her wanted to squeal in triumph, and the other half was desperate to know what would've happened if she hadn't closed the door. But she couldn't let that happen. She would be just another girl to Mack. She knew he never stayed with the same girl long, thanks to their moms' epic gossip sharing. If she slept with Mack, she would get her heart broken all over again, and this time it might not heal.

She changed her clothes quickly but was hesitant to come out. Would he be standing there? Would he be back on the bed or—

"Hurry up, Bailey. I got a room service menu. We should order something."

Room service?

She cracked the door open and saw the tips of his black boots and half of his denim-clad legs on the bed.

"I'm not staying the night with you, Mack. I was just going to pack up and check out." She pushed the door the rest of the way open and did her best not to enjoy the sight of him lounging on the bed.

"Scared of me, Bells?" he teased, his lips curved in an amused grin.

Bells.

She hadn't heard that nickname in forever.

"No. I've never been scared of you," she announced, but he only chuckled.

"Then room service with an old friend shouldn't be a problem."

He was deliberately baiting her, and she should ignore it, but at that moment her stomach growled loudly.

"Fine, let's order. Then after we eat, I need to go."

"Plans with the family tonight?"

"The usual. Mom's got her Christmas cookie swap tomorrow, and I've been enlisted to help bake a billion cookies."

"Nice. I bet my mom's going to do the same."

She sat down on the desk chair and faced him.

"I thought you weren't coming home this year?" She knew he wasn't. It was his year to avoid her.

"Actually, I was planning to be home the entire time. My cousin got engaged a few months ago, and she's having an engagement party at my parents' house on Christmas Eve. So I'm home this year."

They were both going to be home. That surprised her. What if they hadn't met tonight at the fundraiser? Would she have been in her bedroom tomorrow night looking across to his bedroom window expecting it to be dark, only it wouldn't have been? It would've been brightly lit, and she would have seen him in all his grown-up masculine glory. It would have killed her. For so long she'd wanted him, even so small a piece of him as a simple kiss.

Some people lived their whole lives never knowing what it meant to love someone they could never have. But she did. She knew the heartbreaking melancholy of living every second knowing she couldn't have that person. Shakespeare didn't know shit about love. Forget star-crossed. Unrequited love was infinitely worse.

"So, your cousin . . ." She cleared her throat awkwardly.

"Forget about my cousin. Sit down here and pick out your dinner on the menu. Then you and I are going to watch a Christmas movie."

Reject him. Tell him no, sensible Bailey demanded. But sensible Bailey was not in charge. Lovesick Bailey was.

Without a word she sat on the bed, keeping a decent distance between them. She accepted the menu he held out.

"I think I'll take chicken piccata with the lemon orzo pasta."

"Done." Mack lifted the hotel phone off its receiver and dialed room service.

"Two chicken piccatas with the lemon orzo. And a bottle of prosecco with two glasses."

"Prosecco?" Bailey echoed uncertainly as he hung up the phone.

"We're celebrating," Mack said simply, as if she should know what they were celebrating.

"Celebrating what?"

"Us." He grinned that grin that sent flutters to her stomach.

"Us?" It felt ridiculous to keep repeating his words.

"Our first Christmas back together now that we aren't avoiding each other."

Despite his jubilant attitude, his words hit her like a physical blow. He had been avoiding her, just as she had him. To *suspect* it was one thing, but to hear it from his own lips . . . that dropped on her like a hammer.

"Mack, I really don't think this is a good idea." She wanted to say so much more than that, but the words simply wouldn't come.

"We need to do this." He moved a few inches closer to her on the bed.

"Why?"

"Because things have changed. *We've* changed."

She shook her head. "You think you can just walk back into my life? No, I'm not doing this." When she started to get up from the bed, he gently caught her arm and halted her.

"Bailey, we're not kids anymore. It's different now."

"What does that matter? You didn't want me then, so why would you want me now?" She shook his hand off her arm, and when she finally looked at him, she was stunned by the hurt expression on his face.

"Bailey, you were a sixteen-year-old kid. I was eighteen. An adult. I couldn't just . . ." His eyes glowed like winter clouds lit up by lightning. "You touched me, and it was all I had, Bailey, all I had not to . . ."

This was all because of his age? That magical number eighteen had made him so damn noble he'd broken her heart. As a grown woman, she thought it wise, but the teenager she'd once been was still aching from that old wound.

"Are you serious, Mack? That is nuts. You turned eighteen two days before prom. It's—"

He leaned over her and cupped her chin, his lips sealing over hers in a kiss. Their second kiss . . . and it was no less devastatingly perfect than the first. She was vaguely aware of him rolling over her so she lay flat on the bed. Their breaths mingled, and the silence in the room was punctuated only by the sounds their mouths made. He was tender, but there was nothing sweet about his kiss. It was as though he wanted to devour her will to resist him. His tongue sank between her lips, thrusting gently but insistently, reminding her that other parts of him could sink into other parts of her and how good that would feel. His kiss turned hard, then soft, then hard again as though he fought to control himself, to hold back.

That sharp need was with her once again, making her

whimper as he slid one hand down her hip to shape her bottom. She loved his hands. They were large and strong, and when he gripped her bottom, digging his fingers into her, the pleasure-pain of that clinging touch was exquisite. Mack ravaged her mouth, creating a firestorm inside her.

All she could think was that this was what she had always wanted, and it was a thousand times better than she'd ever imagined it would be. Mack wasn't just a good kisser—he was a master kisser. She'd never imagined it would be this incredible to kiss him.

He angled his mouth, somehow deepening the kiss even more. She arched up toward him, her hips rolling, seeking something she didn't have—him inside her.

"Mack." She clutched his shoulders and almost moaned in frustration.

"What do you want, Bailey?"

She shivered in pleasure as he covered her mouth again, not even letting her speak. She liked that he wanted to silence her with kisses. Bailey's head spun with dizzy girlish joy as he leaned more of his weight on top of her. She'd always liked the weight of a lover on her body. It made her feel safe and when she was with a man she trusted, was amazing. There was no question that she trusted Mack with her body. She just didn't trust him with her heart.

"You taste fucking amazing, Bailey." Mack nuzzled her

throat, his soft, hot kisses making her tremble beneath him.

"What are we doing?" she asked in a dazed voice.

"We're just being in the moment," he murmured. His hand slid up under her sweater to trace the lace of her bra before moving to tease the point of one nipple until it was a hardened peak.

"Oh God," she groaned, and he chuckled in her ear.

"Tell me, what do you like? A rough man or a gentle man? I can be anything you want me to be."

It took a moment for her to realize they were talking about sex. Full-on sex. Not just making out.

"Wait . . ." She pushed him away, and he moved back, but not much.

"Are you okay?" Mack asked, genuine concern on his face.

"I . . . yeah. I'm fine. I just wasn't ready for this." She pulled her sweater down the few inches it had ridden up. He placed his hand back on her hip, but the hold was gentle rather than sexual.

"Sorry, I got carried away," he said. "I didn't mean to jump your bones like that."

That shouldn't have hurt her to hear, but strangely it did.

"I'm just going to go back to my own room."

Mack's hand on her hip tightened. "Stay. I'll keep my hands to myself unless you ask me."

The look on his face convinced her. Even though he was dangerous, he was honorable and would keep his promise.

"Fine." She leaned back against the padded headboard, and he did too, the space of a mere foot existing between them. Before that kiss she would've thought that foot was a chasm vaster than the Grand Canyon. Now, though, it felt like he was an inch away and at any second she could be back beneath him on the bed, having what she'd always wanted: him.

He reached for the remote and turned the TV on. He scrolled the channels until he spotted a Christmas movie. *Miracle on 34th Street*. It was her favorite and he knew it, just like he knew *The Polar Express* was her favorite Christmas book. She had once told him as a kid that she still believed in Santa, that there was still magic in the world somewhere and that deep inside she felt he was real. Mack hadn't laughed. He had simply left her a jingle bell in a red velvet box that Christmas night, and she'd stayed up until midnight, shaking it every few minutes to hear it ring. That was who Mack had been. Who was he now? Had adulthood changed Mack into a stranger, or was he still the boy she had loved all her life?

Four

Mack tensed each time Bailey shifted on the bed, his body hyperaware of her as any man would be of a gorgeous woman in such close proximity. But the fact that the woman was Bailey made her much more tempting. With each little movement she made, the teasing floral scent of her hair tickled his nose. He had to stay calm. He had already pushed too hard, too fast, and she had almost walked away. She had no idea how much he really wanted her. If she did, she would have run and slammed the door in his face.

There was nothing stopping him now from having her, not if she wanted him in return. But that was the problem. He didn't know if she wanted him. After what he'd done, breaking her heart, he had no idea how she'd react if he tried to kiss her again. Their lives had diverged so long ago that he wasn't sure their two paths could ever merge again. It was possible he was too late to connect to her again. But he hadn't known this chance would come.

He'd never dreamed she would still be single ten years later. He'd been such an idiot, always trying to ignore his mother whenever she mentioned Bailey because he'd been convinced she was with someone else and he couldn't have handled hearing about it. Now he wished he had pried every detail out of his mother every time they'd spoken about Bailey.

How had no other man tried to lock her down with a large glittering ring and a huge wedding, along with a promise of a joyful life? She deserved that, and there were good men out there who were worthy of her, more worthy than he would ever be.

Mack hadn't been a saint these past ten years. He'd been with women, but none of them had drawn him into a deeper connection. They were fun, nice, intelligent girls, but none of them had touched his heart. There had been a hollowness to his life, like a tree struck by lightning ages ago that still bore a harsh fracture in the wood. He felt burned and lifeless as he looked back on the past ten years and how he'd made them all meaningless because he'd been too afraid to see Bailey.

Not one woman had ever made him feel the way she did. Like he could climb Everest or race the bulls in Spain. She made his future feel limitless. She filled him with a joy that was both wild and peaceful at the same time. He'd feared he would never feel that way again—until he'd seen that cute little bottom of hers in that elf costume as she bent over in front of him. There was no denying the fact that the girl next door would always be the one for him. But he might have wrecked his chances for a brilliant future years ago. Now he was paying for that mistake.

She watched the TV, seemingly completely engrossed in the story of the mysterious man that was on trial for mental competency because he claimed to be the real Santa Claus. It gave him a moment to really see her. Earlier tonight they'd been tending to the children, and then he'd rescued her from those assholes in the bar, but everything had been a flow of constant motion. Now they were still, and he could just breathe and really look at her for the first time in ten years.

God, she was the most beautiful woman he'd ever seen. The slight childhood roundness to her cheeks was gone, and in its place was a face sculpted in soft shapes. Her lips were perfect—neither too plump nor too thin—and her nose had a slight upward curve that hinted at mischief. Her cheekbones were high but not severe, and her heart-shaped face held a natural classical beauty to it that would last her entire life. But it was her eyes that always caught and held him prisoner. Those eyes, such a light shade of brown, like warm melted caramel. He wanted to drown in her eyes. They always peered straight into his head and heart and he felt exposed to her gaze, but he didn't hate the feeling. It made him feel connected to her.

Mack blinked, completely stunned that he'd been just gawking at her like a lovestruck teenager. His gaze shot to the TV screen, and he tried to focus on the movie.

The character Doris Walker spoke: "Faith is believing in things when common sense tells you not to."

Bailey's eyes teared up, and she discreetly tried to wipe her face. She was still a believer in magic, even after all these years. His heart stuttered as memories of her came back to him. There was always this childlike wonder to her. It wasn't naïveté or innocence. It was something more beautiful, something that most people weren't born with. Time hadn't changed the part of her that he loved the most.

When she'd been twelve and he was a worldly fourteen, she'd confessed to him that she still believed in Santa Claus. Something in her eyes that pulled at something in his chest had prevented him from laughing at her, so instead he'd challenged her: If Santa was real, why didn't kids get exactly what they asked for on Christmas? He'd watched as she mulled this over, her lower lip caught between her teeth, and then she'd turned her face up to his, her warm, honey-colored hazel-brown eyes burning with wonder.

"Just because a kid doesn't get their wish for

Christmas doesn't mean there isn't a Santa Claus. Magic requires faith."

He hadn't laughed. He had been almost jealous. What was it like to still believe in magic? He'd supposed most people would assume that a person clinging to such a belief was doing so out of a mental unawareness or a denial of reality. But Bailey? She hadn't been clinging to anything. Her belief had been embedded *inside* her, glowing from within like a light from a hurricane lantern. It could never be snuffed out.

Now, he could see by her face that she hadn't changed. Whatever she had done in the last decade, she hadn't lost that ability to believe in magic.

"Bailey—" He wasn't sure what he'd planned to say, so he was intensely relieved when a knock on the door interrupted him.

He answered the door, and a hotel employee rolled the cart into the room with their dinner. Mack instructed the man where to set up the food. Bailey took her tray and retreated to the part of the bed by the headboard, and Mack joined her after he saw the man out the door. He poured two glasses of prosecco, and they ate their dinner. The movie entered a lull, and he had a moment to speak to her without feeling like he was distracting her.

"So, what have you been up to? Fill me in on the last ten years."

Her startled eyes flicked to his, and he instantly

regretted asking her when he noticed a wariness and sadness in their depths.

She sipped her drink and turned thoughtful, as though carefully planning what to say. "I went to Columbia University in New York and got a degree in graphic design."

It was useful information, but he got the sense she was avoiding a more personal discussion, and she had every right to. He no longer deserved to hear about that part of her life. He would take what he could get and learn as much as he could about her.

"What do you like about graphic design?" He was driven by a desperate need to fill in the blanks of this grown-up Bailey, to know what she loved, what got her up in the morning, what her plans for the rest of her life were.

"It's like I have the world at my fingertips. The things I can do with images—it's like magic."

Mack's lips curved. *Magic.* It always came back to magic with her.

"What I really want—" She halted, and her face flushed red.

"What do you really want?"

"I want to be able to do amazing things like book cover designs. Knowing your images can sit on a thousand people's bookshelves or e-reader libraries, and you can bring an author's book to life . . . someday I would love to run a book cover design company." Her face lit with excitement as she spoke, and he loved seeing how passionate she was about this career option.

"Have you created any covers yet?" He had never really thought about book covers being a huge source of design work, but it made sense now that he thought about it.

"I have in my spare time. I've even done a few mock-ups."

"Can I see them?"

"You want to?" Her light brown brows arched up over her stunning eyes.

"Definitely."

She slipped her phone out of her pocket and swiped around her online cloud files before she turned the screen to face him.

"This one I did for a thriller." She walked him through the elements of her design, and he nodded, listening raptly as she showed that she really knew her craft.

"Show me another," he insisted. She moved closer and showed him a fantasy cover of a woman in a yellow ball gown with a dark castle behind her, half in shadow, roses surrounding the edge of the art.

"It's a 'Beauty and the Beast' retelling," she explained.

"I definitely got the fairy-tale vibe. The rose elements framing it are a nice touch."

"You think?"

He nodded. "So you plan to open a design studio. I

bet you could run that on the side while you work at Trouble Inc. Andrews doesn't have strict noncompete clauses, especially since we're not in the book business."

"I have been thinking about my options. If I started now, I could build it up over time, if I could make a decent number of covers for clients. The challenge would be to break into the business and find clients. What about you?" She pushed her finished tray away and fixed him with a meaningful stare.

"Me?"

"Yeah, what's the infamous Mack up to?"

"I'm infamous now?" He couldn't hold back a laugh.

She grinned a little mysteriously. "You've always been infamous."

"Good to know." He tipped his head back, staring at the ceiling. "I've been focused. A lot of work on corporate headquarter designs."

"And you've been traveling," she added.

"I have. But there are still a lot of places I want to see." He had spent more than a few holidays on the other side of the world, much to his family's displeasure, but it was necessary. He'd had to avoid Bailey. He'd been convinced that he would not have been able to see her marching up the steps to her parents' house with a handsome husband and children in tow. It would have broken something inside him, and he didn't want to think about why she made him feel that way.

"What's Christmas like on a beach?" Bailey asked with a laugh.

"Different," he chuckled. "There are a lot of half-naked Santas running around."

"Ooh, were there sexy Santas?" she asked hopefully.

"A few, but mostly the chubby older white bearded guys. I think I miss Christmas snow the most. At least at home there's usually snow on the ground."

"Speaking of snow . . ." Bailey suddenly pointed at the hotel room window, her eyes widening. "When did it become a blizzard out there?"

"Holy shit." He got up from the bed and looked out the window at the massive white cloud of snow that was covering the parking lot. The lot had dozens of light poles to show the parking spaces, and swirls of snow created golden orbs around the lights.

"When did that start?" Bailey murmured from beside him.

"Must've been during the fundraiser party."

Bailey's cell phone suddenly rang, and she rushed to answer.

"Hey, Mom . . . Wait, what did you say?"

Mack spun, listening to Bailey.

"The highway's closed," she whispered to him before speaking to her mother again. "Power outages? Mom, I should—oh . . . ." She shot a worried glance at Mack. "Okay, Mom, call me in the morning."

She hung up. "Everyone in the neighborhood lost power. Your parents' house and mine. The major roads and the highways are also closed. She said she would call with an update in the morning."

Damn, that sounded grim. Suddenly, what she'd said just clicked. Baily was trapped in the hotel because of the snow. Trapped with *him*.

"Sounds like you definitely need to stay the night *here*."

Her face turned red. "Next door. I need to stay next door," she said. "Which is where I should go now." She collected the pieces of her elf costume and dropped them into the shopping bag before heading to the door. In a mere moment, she would be gone from his life again if he didn't stop her.

"Bailey." Mack was there, stopping her by placing a hand against the door, using his weight to keep it closed. Their eyes locked, and the air between them seemed to get sucked out of the room.

"*Mack*." Her tone held a mix of worry and pleading.

He swallowed hard at the way she said his name, as though she needed something, but he wasn't sure what to give her.

"I'm here if you need me . . . for anything." He wanted to say so much more, but he felt anything else would be unwelcome to her.

"Thanks . . . maybe I'll see you later." But he heard the *goodbye* in those words.

She turned the doorknob, and he stepped back, letting her go. As she entered the hall, he tried one more time to say what lay in his heart.

"I wish I had kissed you that night after prom."

She half turned, her eyes holding his briefly. "I wish you had too." Then she let the door close.

He stayed by the shut door, letting her walk away, his eyes closed he tried to fight off a sudden wave of dark emotion, which broke upon the bitter shores of his heart. She had wanted to give him everything back then, but the gift of Bailey was long gone. He threw himself down on the bed and stared at the ceiling for a long while. Half an hour later, the power in the hotel died and darkness fell around him.

"Shit," he groaned. It was going to be a long, cold night.

Bailey had just stepped out of the shower when the electricity shut off.

"What the hell?" She scrambled for a towel in the near pitch-black bathroom. Her fingers brushed against the fluffy fabric of the towel she had set on the counter. With a little shiver, she wrapped it around her body and exited the bathroom.

Pale moonlight obscured mostly by the snow barely lit the hotel room enough for her to find her underwear and the flannel pajamas that she had packed. The bottoms were shorts rather than long pants and she knew she would get cold fast if the hotel's power didn't come back on soon.

Bailey attempted to dry her hair with one of the smaller towels, but she knew it was going to end up in a rumpled, wavy mass without a hair dryer. But the worst part was the wet hair was going to make her insanely cold. She dove under the blankets of her bed and tried to get some sleep. But after an hour, with her teeth chattering and no sign of the power coming back on, she gave up. There was only one thing she could think of to keep warm, and it was such a bad idea.

She grabbed her cell phone and room key and went to Mack's door. She stared at it for what felt like forever. When she couldn't put it off anymore because her bones were rattling from the cold, she knocked. He opened the door, and she took in the sight of him barefoot, wearing blue jeans and a black T-shirt, beneath the glow of the red emergency lights in the hallway, his hair mussed. His face was relaxed until he realized it was her, and then he tensed.

"Bailey? What's the matter? Are you okay?"

"Y-yeah." She tried to keep her teeth from chattering

—she was freezing. "So, the power's out. And, well, I am freezing and I thought we could help each other stay warm . . . Oh God, this is so stupid," she muttered to herself, her cheeks on fire.

"What?" he asked, disbelieving, but she knew in her bones that he wasn't misunderstanding what she was suggesting.

"Nothing." She started to turn away, her pulse racing in her ears as his decade-long rejection played out in an instant in her mind's eye. She had to get away, find another way to keep warm, and try not to think of his solid warm body and drugging kisses a room away.

She shivered as he caught her. One hand curled around her bare arm, and her flesh prickled with awareness as her stomach dropped at the pressure of his strong, wonderfully warm fingers.

"Come in and warm up," he whispered, each word igniting hope inside her. "We have no idea when the power will be back on. We should do what we can to keep warm."

She stared at him for a moment as he stood bathed in the snow-obscured moonlight. The shadows on his face were too dark to see his eyes properly, but she knew they blazed with the same intent she remembered from ten years ago. But this time, he was reaching out to her, not pulling away.

She swallowed as she made up her mind. "Thanks."

She slipped past him, their bodies brushing in the dark, and the friction made her breath catch and her nipples pebble.

The door closed behind her, and she paused, letting him step up behind her, the warmth of his body a scant inch from hers, warming the minimal space between them with heat.

"Mack . . . ," she said with uncertainty and stopped.

"Bailey?" Her name, whispered in the dark in his deep voice, obliterated the last of her good sense.

"If we do this . . . ," she began, and her mind screamed the correction *When we do this*. "It's just tonight. We go back to our lives tomorrow, and we never speak of this again."

She held her breath, waiting, and for an agonizing moment he said nothing. Then he spun her to face him. They came together in a kiss that was brighter and hotter than any distantly burning star in the winter sky. Her pulse raced wildly as he pushed her back up against the wall. When he kissed her like this, everything she had ever felt for him came back, like lightning striking her. Electricity shot down her limbs, and she gasped against his mouth. He cupped the back of her head and caged her against the wall, leaving no doubt that he was in charge of this, in charge of her.

"Wanted this so much," he murmured against her lips. "Had so many fantasies about you, Bailey." He was no poet, but the desire in his voice was the best love song she'd ever heard, and the feel of his desperate hands rubbing at her pajamas was purely animalistic. She kicked out of her pajama bottoms and squealed as he suddenly lifted her in his arms. Her legs wrapped around his waist, and he carried her to the bed. Somehow, her button-up pajama top slipped away, leaving her in her panties as he laid her back on his bed.

He stripped off his T-shirt, exposing his chest. Everything else beyond him seemed to vanish in the darkness, and only they were illuminated by the nearby window that let the snow-softened moonlight through. It was easier to surrender to her fantasies when she was in the dark with him. She could pretend it was a dream and there would be no heartbreak tomorrow.

She had seen him half-naked plenty of times from her bedroom window growing up, but that had been the slim-muscled body of a seventeen-year-old boy. Now he was broader in the shoulders, his muscles more harshly cut beneath his skin. Her own body screamed to touch his, to run her tongue over every magnificent groove and curve of those gorgeous muscles.

"Fuck, Bailey," he groaned. "You're gorgeous. Too beautiful to be real." He stared down at her as though lost in the same wild, lustful thoughts as she was. It lasted for a single moment, and the intensity seemed to build, and she couldn't bear it.

"Touch me, then. Prove you're real too," she challenged.

With a darkly primal grin, he knelt at her feet and pulled her toward him. She parted her thighs, and he reached up, fisting his hand in her panties. Then he tore the scrap of lace from her body. The flimsy cloth snapped beneath his grip, and she whimpered at the sudden flood of wet heat between her thighs at his roughness. She didn't want the boy next door—she wanted the grown man who could fuck her hard enough to make her forget the past and cease to worry about the future.

In the dim, pale moonlight, she saw Mack's gray eyes glowed as he forced her thighs wider and he leaned in, his lips trailing up her leg with light kisses toward her core.

She'd had a few boyfriends go down on her, but none had affected her the way Mack did. He licked her like a man starved, his tongue lapping at her, which only made her wetter.

"Have you been naughty or nice this year, Bailey?" he asked before he dragged his tongue through her slit, and she saw actual stars as she threw her head back.

"Oh God," she gasped. "Naughty . . . *definitely* naughty."

He laughed, his warm breath tickling her.

"A bad girl, eh?" He slipped a finger into her, pushing it slowly deeper, making her all too aware that he was gently owning her body.

"Uh-huh . . ." She was panting now. Her mind had only one goal: pleasure. That was all that mattered. Mind-blowing pleasure. She knew Mack could give it to her.

He slowly withdrew his finger from her core and stood up, leaning over her. "Suck it," he commanded in a dark tone that sent delicious shivers through her.

She parted her lips, and he slid his finger into her mouth. She tasted herself on him, and it made her legs tremble and close at the sinful action. She let him remove his finger from her mouth, and it escaped from her lips with a soft pop.

"Do you know what bad girls get for Christmas?" he asked.

"A lump of coal?" she answered cheekily.

He opened his jeans and pushed them down, his hard cock jutting out toward her.

"Spread your thighs again, *brat*," Mack growled, but there was such affection in the word *brat* that it came across as an endearment, so she complied with even more hunger for him. He snagged his jeans from the floor, removed a foil packet, and tore it open. She watched him roll the condom over his hard cock, and she swallowed in anticipation of being filled by him.

Mack bent over the bed and crawled up over her body. Pinning her down on the bed, he settled his weight on top of her, and she did as he ordered, her legs spreading wide. He braced himself above her, his thick forearms on either side of her head. He shifted, reaching down between them, gripping his shaft, and then he was entering her. She moaned at the sudden hard invasion. He was almost too big—she wasn't even sure she could take him.

"That's it, take it, baby," he murmured in her ear. "Don't be quiet. Let me hear you scream with pleasure."

When he withdrew and slammed back in, she did scream. It felt so good and almost overwhelming at the same time, and she couldn't keep her mouth shut. Pure sex glowed in his gray eyes as he stared down at her.

"You want to be my dirty little secret, Bailey?" he asked as he pummeled his hips against hers. The sound of their flesh slapping in the silent hotel room mixed with their shared breaths was an erotic symphony that she would remember for the rest of her life.

"Yes." She could barely speak. She was so lost in him and the reality of Mack owning this last part of her.

"You know how often I've dreamed of this? Of sinking myself into this sweet little body?"

She couldn't speak now. It was impossible. Mack was a dirty talker, and she loved it.

"Ever since I left for college, you were all I could think about. I wanted to hear you scream my name." His low, rough confession as he made love to her, had her head spinning.

She gasped, breathing out his name in pants.

"You're my pretty toy, aren't you?"

His wicked words were spinning this into a new level of eroticism that was almost too perfect. She whimpered as he changed the angle of his thrusts.

The man was a sex god. He knew exactly what to do, how to brush her clit as he circled his hips and then changed his rhythm. It took her a moment to realize he was keeping her from coming.

"Mack, please," she begged.

His rough chuckle only made her wetter. "My girl wants to come?"

She bit her lip and nodded frantically. "Please."

"Come for me, baby," he urged. and he deepened his thrusts, unleashing his sexual fury on her, and it was exactly what she needed. The orgasm nearly caused her to black out. Her heart actually stuttered to a stop. Mack thrust several more times, almost brutally, taking his pleasure from her sated, limp body, and then he called out her name like it was the most important thing he could ever say and emptied himself inside her. He stilled above her, their eyes locking in the snowy darkness as they shared shaky breaths.

What they'd done . . . they couldn't take it back, and she feared it was the most wonderful mistake of her life.

Mack held still above Bailey, his heart battering against his ribs. He had completely lost his mind and his self-control. He had just fucked the cute little girl next door like she was some sort of personal pleasure toy, and it had been the most amazing thing he had ever felt in his life.

"God, Bailey, are you okay? I didn't mean to get so—" He wasn't sure why he was whispering, considering how loud they had just been. The whole hotel probably heard them.

"Don't you dare apologize," Bailey whispered back.

"I just treated you like—"

"We just released a decade of fantasies together," she said. "It was bound to happen."

Bound to happen? Why was she reducing the hottest sex in his life to the pent-up frustrations of teenagers?

"Stop trying to lessen what just happened, Bailey. There were two of us in this bed."

At this, she looked away from him. He moved off her, their bodies separating. She slipped off the bed and disappeared into the bathroom. Mack sat naked on the bed, staring around at the darkened, powerless hotel room with the snow still swirling outside. Then he retrieved his briefs from the floor and Bailey's torn panties and pajamas. When he tried the bathroom door, he found it unlocked. She was in the dark, running water over her hands.

"Here," he murmured and gave her the clothes.

"Thanks." She took them and dressed in the dark

while he cleaned himself and slipped his briefs back on. She stared at the ripped lace panties and then with a sigh tossed them into the bathroom trash can. He'd never done that before, gotten so dominant that he'd ripped a woman's panties clean off her body. Looking at her now, though, he was afraid his sexual aggression might have been too much for her. Had he crossed a line?

"Are you really okay?" He caught her by the shoulders. He had to know if he had done something terribly wrong.

"Why . . . yes." She sounded so unsure that it crushed his chest in a viselike grip, making it hard to breathe.

"Bailey, talk to me. Please, you're scaring the hell out of me."

She lifted her face to his, and he cursed the darkness for not letting him see her better.

"It's just . . . I've wanted that, wanted you for as long as I can remember. Now that I've had you—part of you—"

Mack held his breath when she stopped talking, terrified of what she might say next. Was the *idea* of him was better than the reality? He couldn't compete with a dream version of himself.

"You're *so much better* than I ever imagined, and I know it won't last. It can't last."

He wanted to ask her why it couldn't, but he didn't dare. He had no right to ask that.

"So we have tonight," he replied, pulling her into his

arms. "I'll be whatever you want, do whatever you want. I'm yours until dawn."

This seemed to be what she wanted to hear. She relaxed into him at these words, and he kissed the crown of her hair. She was warm now, but the room was still too cold.

"Come back to bed. It's chilly." He pulled back the covers, and she climbed into bed. He joined her, spooning her into his body and wrapping himself around her.

"I'm so tired, but I don't think I can sleep," she murmured.

"Let's talk," he suggested. "Let me have a chance to get to know the new grown-up Bailey."

She laughed at this, the sound an adorable sleepy giggle. "Do I get access to all the grown-up Mack secrets?"

"Absolutely," he promised.

"Okay, ask away."

And he did. He asked every question he'd wanted to know over the years. Her favorite college classes, what she did when she wasn't at work, was her favorite color still that bright green?

She asked him about his trips, the islands that he'd visited, the places in Europe that had given him inspiration.

"I want to see the world like you," she said with a yawn. "I've always stayed close to home . . . I don't know why."

He had known she'd never really traveled far from where they'd grown up. The years that she had missed the few Christmas events when their paths would have crossed, she'd never even left the city, yet she had still been just out of his reach.

"You could come with me next time," he suggested. "Next year I think I want to go to Germany for the Christmas markets."

She stopped breathing for a few heartbeats.

"That would be lovely," she admitted, but he heard the false joy in her tone. She wasn't actually agreeing to come. She was just pretending to entertain the thought. But why? He nuzzled her neck and pressed a soft kiss to her skin below her ear, and she shivered in his arms.

"Thank you, Mack," she whispered.

"For what?" He held her closer, drawing the blankets up tighter around their bodies.

"For this, for tonight. It was a wonderful Christmas present."

He didn't respond. His throat was too tight. She drifted off to sleep, and all he could do was lie awake. He didn't want to miss a second of this night with her because he knew that come morning, she would run from him.

Five

The power was back on when Bailey stirred the next morning. She stretched and yawned, feeling well rested. A hard, warm male body was next to her in the bed, and in a flash she remembered what had happened last night. She covered her face with her hands, not knowing whether to laugh or shake her head at herself.

Mack lay beside her still asleep, illuminated by the bright sunlight reflecting off the snow outside. The bands of light bathed his bare upper body where he had stretched out in the night and caused the covers to fall down to his hips.

Bailey bit her lip and smiled at him. She had never seen him like this before. Sleep softened him in a way she'd never seen before. His golden hair fell against his closed eyes, and his lips curved ever so slightly, as though whatever he dreamed about was wonderful. Last night had been intense and perfect. To be with him, and just experience it all, had been incredible. But it was over. She had to let go because she wouldn't risk her heart, not again. Mack wasn't going to settle down anytime soon, and she was ready for that next step in life—marriage, kids, all of it.

I got you out of my system, Mack. Once and for all.

She slipped out of bed, careful not to wake him. Then she left his room and tiptoed down the hall to her own. She took a quick shower, dried her hair and changed into a warm winter outfit before she called her mom.

"The power's back on, thank God. I've been on the phone with Judy Macholan."

Mack's mom?

"How are the roads?" Bailey tried to change the subject.

"Decent. The snowplows were out all night. Your father went to the store an hour ago and said it was pretty clear to drive. I think you can make it from your hotel."

"Okay. I should be home in less than an hour." She hung up and quickly packed her suitcase and headed downstairs to check out of the hotel.

As she paid her bill, she saw one of the men who had been making sexist comments at her from the bar last night. He didn't recognize her now, though. She walked straight toward him as he prepared his coffee from the lobby bar. With perfect execution, she bumped into him, and he hissed as the scalding-hot cup he'd been about to put a lid on splattered all over his chest, ruining his dress shirt.

"Oh God, I'm so sorry," she cooed falsely and patted his chest with a single napkin, nonchalantly smearing coffee about. He glared at her.

"This was a three-hundred-dollar shirt," he growled.

"Was it?" she replied, faking her best innocent look. She didn't miss the wedding band on his finger. "Better be careful—your wife might stuff your stocking full of coal if she knew how you treated Santa's elves."

Bailey burned the stupid expression on his face into her mind as she wheeled her suitcase out the door, trying not to laugh. As it turned out, her mother was right. The roads were clear, and she was able to get home in forty-five minutes. When she got out of the car, she saw Mack's mom at the Macholans' mailbox.

"Bailey! You're home!" Judy greeted and tramped toward her in the snow.

"Mrs. Macholan, how are you?" Bailey had to control the sudden flare of panic. She felt like she had the words *I slept with your son* painted on her forehead.

"Great! I heard from your mother that you're working at Trouble Inc. Did your mother tell you that Mack works at Trouble Inc. too? He's in the engineering department." Judy was positively beaming as she shared that.

"Oh? I didn't know," she lied. "Small world, huh?" She removed her suitcase from her trunk.

"Definitely small," Judy agreed. "He's home this year too. It would be fun for you two to catch up. You were always so close as kids."

"We were, but you know how things go. You grow up and grow apart."

Judy's lips quivered slightly, and she tried to smile.

"Bailey, what happened between you? You and Mack just stopped hanging out after prom, and I was worried . . . well, that something happened."

Bailey wanted this conversation to end, and decided if she told Mack's mom the truth it would put an end to their mothers' scheming.

"Nothing happened, Mrs. Macholan, and that's the problem."

Judy's eyes widened in sudden understanding. "Oh . . ."

"Well, um . . . Merry Christmas, Mrs. Macholan."

"Merry Christmas, Bailey. Tell your mother we'll see you all tonight."

"Okay. Wait, what?" Bailey halted and faced Judy.

"You're coming over to our house for Christmas Eve. Jenna is here for her engagement party and wanted to have you all come over. So, we've invited you all."

Crap . . . Mack and I are going to have to see each other tonight?

Judy smiled hesitantly. "Mack will be here tonight. Is that okay?"

"It is," Bailey assured her smoothly.

"Well, good. I hope you have a fun time tonight. Your mom and I wanted to have Christmas Eve together like we had when you were kids."

"I'm looking forward to it," Bailey said.

"Well, don't let me keep you. It's cold out here, so go on and we'll see you tonight."

Bailey rolled her suitcase up to the front door and rang the doorbell. Her father answered, grinning as he pulled her into his arms. He was a tall, well-built man in his sixties with eyes like hers, a warm shade of hazel-brown.

"Bailey, you survived the blackout?"

"I did," she laughed. "The hotel had no power half the night. But we were okay."

"*We?*" Her father caught on to the word she let slip out.

"Yeah . . . the other hotel guests," she covered quickly.

"Right . . . Well, come and help your mother. She's elbow-deep in cookie dough and in desperate need of rein-forcements."

"How did you escape cookie duty?" she asked as her dad lifted her suitcase inside the house and rolled it toward the stairs for her.

"I'm late setting up my train." He winked and nodded

at the mess of train tracks in a heap by the Christmas tree in the living room.

"Nice. Do you need me to help?" Bailey whispered conspiratorially.

"Honey, is that Bailey?" her mother called from the kitchen.

"Yeah, Mom, it's me." She shrugged out of her tan knee-length wool coat and tried not to laugh when her father gave her a mock salute and turned toward his train set.

Bailey found her mom in the kitchen, frantically loading up a tray of cookie dough balls on the still-hot cookie sheet. The bar countertop dividing the kitchen from the family room was covered in plates of sugar cookies, crackles, peanut butter kiss cookies, and gingerbread snaps. Flour and sugar dusted the surfaces of the island and the counter by the oven.

"Open the oven for me," her mother ordered as she dropped the last ball of cookie dough on the cookie sheet then carried the tray toward the oven.

Bailey opened the door for her mother, who placed the cookies in the oven.

"Set the timer for thirteen minutes, and I'll get the next batch ready," her mother said.

Relieved, Bailey settled into the mode of prepping cookies. It was nice to have something to do with her hands, and it was a busy enough task that her mind couldn't stay completely fixed on Mack and how she had left him alone in bed this morning. Whenever she and her mother had a brief pause, thoughts of Mack came rushing back.

"I talked to Judy when I got here," she said to her mother.

"Oh?"

"Uh-huh. Apparently, we're going over there tonight for Christmas Eve dinner?"

"Yes," her mother said and shot her a look. "That's okay with you, right?"

"Yeah, of course," Bailey replied with a pretend smile.

"Good, because Mack is home this year. It's been too long since you've seen him. It will be good for you to catch up."

"For sure." Bailey kept quiet while her mom shared updates on all their neighbors.

"Mr. McGinty is going to be in *A Christmas Carol* this year at the community theater."

"Old grumpy McGinty?" She choked on a laugh. She and Mack used to throw water balloons at him and steal the strawberries that he grew every year in his garden.

"Yes, and we have tickets for it this evening after dinner."

"Can we have a Christmas some year where we just stay at home?" Bailey sighed. She wasn't up to all the society events, not this year.

Her mother rolled her eyes. "We are staying at home. It's just one party and one play. I think you'll survive."

Four hours later, Bailey was up in her childhood bedroom digging through the old box of decorations that were hers, ones that she'd put up in her bedroom.

"Mom?" she called down the stairs.

"Yes, dear?" Her mother's head appeared at the foot of the stairs.

"Where is my old jingle bell? The one in the velvet box?"

"The one Mack gave you?"

"Yeah." She stared at the storage tub of old strings of lights and ornaments.

"It should be in the box."

Bailey dug around until she found it at the very bottom and lifted the old velvet box up and opened it. The large silver jingle bell was nestled in the velvet. She lifted it up and gave it a good shake. Nothing happened. It was silent. *Broken*. A quiet despair filled Bailey's chest as she gave it another shake, but still no sound came through. It was like the last of her happy childhood memories had died with the loss of the bell's sound.

She slumped down on the bed and after a moment put the bell back in the box and closed the lid.

The house phone rang, and a moment later her mother called up the stairs.

"Bailey, phone for you!"

Bailey put the velvet box on her nightstand, got up and called back down to her mother.

"Who is it?"

"It's Mack!" her mother shouted back.

Mack was calling her? She picked up the house phone from its charging cradle on her desk and answered it.

"Hello?"

"Turn around, Bells," Mack's deep voice said. She turned around so she faced her window, and across the fifteen feet that separated their houses she saw Mack standing in his old bedroom, smirking at her as he held his own house phone to his ear. He looked sexy in a pair of blue jeans and a loose cream colored fisherman's sweater.

"I can't believe you still remember this number," she said, unable to hide a smile.

"I think I dialed this number more than my own as a kid. Hell, one time I woke your parents up after a party when I needed a ride home. I was too drunk to realize I'd called your house, not mine. Your dad actually showed up to come get me. He never told my parents."

"What party was that?" Bailey asked.

"Andrew Givens's party. I was only sixteen. You were still in middle school."

"Oh, right." God, those two years between them had felt like a century back then.

"Anyway," he chuckled. "I didn't have your cell phone number, and I thought it would be a good idea to continue this conversation where our moms might not eavesdrop."

They were fifteen feet apart, yet it felt like he was standing right in front of her, his voice in her ear, and she could almost imagine the feel of his warm, hard body against hers . . .

Heat suffused her face. "Yeah, good idea." She gave him her cell number, and then they both hung up their house phones. She stood there, staring at him as he dialed her number on his cell. Then he put his phone to his ear and came toward the window and braced his arms on the windowsill. He gazed at her, and she couldn't look away as she pulled her cell phone out of her back pocket and answered it.

"Now, let's talk about this morning," he said softly, more seductively. She stared at his lips as they moved, all too aware of what those lips and tongue could do to her.

God, this man was *always* going to be catnip to her, wasn't he? And now that she knew what it was like to be his . . . it was even harder to deny the pleasure he could give her.

"What about this morning?" She went to her own window and leaned against it, staring back at him.

"I've decided I'm not done with *us*."

Her heartbeat ticked up in excitement, and she sucked in a breath.

"Us?" she repeated.

"Yeah. Last night was too damn good. Why give us only one night? Why not give us another couple of nights? Then . . . we can go back to our separate lives."

"So, what, we sneak around? You think our mothers won't figure it out?" she challenged, but damn him, he was right. She wanted more of them too; she didn't want to be done either. It was a bad idea, but she couldn't find it in her to care enough to be sensible when it came to him now that she knew what it felt like to be with him.

"That depends. Can you be quiet?" His whispered voice was in her ear, sending delicious chills down her spine and waking up every feminine part of her. "I love it when you scream, but I might just have to put my hand over your mouth while I fuck you." He continued to stare at her, hunger making his silver eyes glow.

Bailey drew in a shaky breath. "Let me think about it." But as she hung up, she felt her body had already made the decision. They both stared at each other for a long moment, the distance between them infinite and yet too close. His gaze wandered leisurely up and down her body, and she wondered how many times he'd looked toward her window as a teenager like she had his. He put his cell phone in his jeans pocket, and with a promising look and a rakish wink at her, he left his boyhood bedroom and turned out the light.

Holy hell . . . Her stocking was going to be stuffed to the brim with coal.

Mack chuckled to himself as he left his bedroom. He had definitely affected her. That was good, because after waking up this morning and finding himself alone in bed, he had taken her leaving as a blow to his ego. Hell, more than that, he'd been hurt, and he didn't like admitting that. He'd never had a woman try to escape his bed that fast the following morning. Usually, he was the one sneaking off before breakfast. But *she'd* snuck out on him. So he was going to give her sweet, delicious torture until she admitted that last night wasn't enough.

He headed downstairs and found his mom putting the finishing touches on the large dining room table. His cousin Jenna was helping her.

"Hey, little cuz," he greeted and hugged her. "When did you get here?"

"About five minutes ago. Rob is outside with Uncle Mike."

"Oh? Introduce me?" he asked with an evil grin.

Jenna laughed and punched him in the shoulder. "Only if you behave. He's wonderful, and I don't want you scaring him off before the wedding."

Mack crossed his finger in an X shape over his heart. "I'll be good." He did, however, vow silently to assess this "Rob" because Jenna was his favorite cousin. Her mother, Maggie, and his mother, Judy, were sisters only a year apart, and Jenna had spent most of her summers with Mack's family after her father died when she was twelve. She was Bailey's age, and they had gotten along really well.

He followed Jenna outside, where Mack's father, Mike, and a man around Mack's age stood. A set of reindeer that would light up at night lay on the snow-covered lawn in the backyard by the storage shed.

"Rob, this is my cousin, Montgomery." She nodded at the dark-haired man beside Mack's father.

Mack held out a hand. "Everyone calls me Mack."

"Rob Harrison. Nice to meet you." Rob shook Mack's hand.

"I'll leave you boys to it," Jenna said, then paused. "Hey, Mack, is Bailey coming over tonight? I told your mom to invite the Willis family."

"Er, yeah, she is," Mack replied.

"Good. I miss that girl." Jenna grinned and headed inside.

"Who is Bailey?" Rob asked.

"*Who is Bailey?*" Mack's dad chuckled. "She's Mack's other half."

Mack glared at his father.

"Really?" Rob smiled as he obviously sensed he was being let in on an inside family joke.

"Yep. Childhood sweethearts, those two. Not sure why they've been avoiding each other the last few years. Seems silly, if you ask me."

Mack inwardly winced. His father had definitely noticed way too much. Mack had never really thought about whether his avoidance of Bailey had been obvious to his family or not. He'd always spun elaborate tales every other year about how the trip he was taking was best done in December, either for smaller crowds or cheaper travel costs.

"So, what's with the reindeer?" Mack asked his dad in a somewhat brusque tone.

"Oh, we're going to put them up in the front yard." His father waved vaguely toward the house. "Your mother thought they would be cute or something. I think she just wants the men out of the way so she, Jenna, and Maggie can talk wedding plans."

"Don't you need to be in there, Rob?" Mack asked.

"Nope," Rob chuckled. "Whatever Jenna wants is what I want too."

"Smart man." Mack's father slapped Rob on the back. "Now, let's go set these up."

The three of them carried the reindeer to the front yard and were nearly finished setting them up when an old man in his Sunday best tweed suit strolled by them on the sidewalk. He was a slightly rotund man, with a pale grayish beard that touched his collarbones.

"McGinty! Merry Christmas! Can't wait to see you tonight!" Mack's father waved at the old man. McGinty nodded politely, waved his walking cane at them, and continued toward his house.

"Jenna said you guys used to pull pranks on him," Rob said with a laugh.

"Only a little. We mostly stole the vegetables and fruits he grew in his garden." Mack frowned, realizing how stupid it sounded saying that out loud as an adult.

"So he's going to be in some Christmas play we're going to tonight?" Rob asked Mack as they finished plugging in the last of the reindeer's power cords to the extension cord that ran from the house.

"I think he's supposed to play Ebenezer Scrooge in *A Christmas Carol* tonight." Mack turned his head and out of the corner of his eye caught sight of something moving. He stilled and stared at Bailey. She was standing in front of the big picture window in their living room, hanging an ornament on the tree. She wore a red-and-black Buffalo plaid dress that came down to mid-thigh. Her light brown hair bounced in soft curls against her back and shoulders as she moved.

God, she was the most beautiful thing he'd ever seen.

"Who's that?" Rob asked.

"That is the infamous *Bailey*." Mack's father chuckled again.

Mack stood outside for a long moment, drinking in the sight of her before he went back into his own house. He was going to find a way to get her alone tonight.

Six

Bailey stepped into the Macholans' house later that night, following her parents. The place was decorated for Christmas in every room and music filled the entryway. The scent of cinnamon and cookies danced all the way from the Macholan kitchen to the front part of the house. A pang of longing hit her hard. This place had been a second home once. She'd lived here almost as much as she had at her own home. Nothing had really changed, except a few updated furniture pieces. It was still the warm, welcoming home of the Macholan clan.

A swell of nerves made her feel almost shaky. How were she and Mack going to get through this tonight and not let anyone figure out they were doing . . . well . . . whatever they were doing? The house was filled to the brim with Macholan relatives and family friends who were there to celebrate the holidays and Jenna's engagement. Bailey studied every face close to her, seeking Mack, but she didn't see him. That filled her with a mixture of relief and disappointment.

"Bailey!" a familiar female voice squealed. Bailey looked up to see Jenna rushing down the staircase toward her. Jenna was a gorgeous blonde with deep blue eyes and a bright smile. She looked absolutely dazzling in a knee-length green cocktail dress.

"Jenna!" She hugged her old childhood friend.

"Congratulations!" Jenna said.

"What for? Shouldn't I be saying that to you?" Bailey asked in confusion.

"Thanks, but I owe you a congratulations. You have completely thrown Mack off his game. He's been flustered all day, and I believe you have something to do with it, because every time someone mentions you, he goes all red in the face. It's the best thing I've ever seen." Jenna grinned wickedly. "So, what did you do to him?"

"*Do* to him?" Bailey was hung up on the idea of Mack being flustered by her.

"Yes, you clearly did something this year. I've asked about you each Christmas since high school, and he's always been able to smoothly distract me. Not this year. Something is different."

"Well, maybe it's because we haven't seen each other

in so long, and it's just bound to be awkward now that we're both home."

"But you saw each other last night . . ." Jenna's brows knit together.

"No, we—"

Jenna held up her phone, showing a picture of Bailey and Mack standing by the Santa's village. "This was posted on Trouble Inc.'s social media profiles. Rob found it. Don't know how the moms haven't seen it yet."

Bailey stared at the photo, marveling at how she and Mack looked as they handed out presents together.

"So cute, right? Did you guys plan that?"

Bailey shook her head and handed Jenna her phone back.

"We haven't seen each other since he graduated, at least not really. This was the first time we'd spoken in ten years. We were volunteered for the positions by our department heads at the party, not knowing the other would get picked."

"Wow, small world to end up at the same company and then the whole Santa thing."

Small indeed, Bailey thought.

"So are you guys like, finally . . . *you know* . . . ," Jenna whispered.

Bailey felt like she was in high school all over again.

"No, definitely not."

"No?" Jenna pouted in disappointment. "Damn. I had hoped . . . You've been the only girl he's ever talked about, even after all this time." She nibbled her lip. "So if you guys aren't . . . then are you dating someone right now?"

"Nope. There was a guy a few months ago, but it was more of a fun thing, nothing serious."

"So you're single?" Jenna's eyes lit up with a mixture of hope and mischief. "We really need to catch up. Why the hell haven't we gotten together in the last few years?" Jenna asked. "I could have been setting you up with some quality guys, and you could have gone on double dates with Rob and me."

"Oh no . . . don't get any ideas," Bailey protested with a laugh. God, she'd missed her friend more than she'd realized. She'd been so focused on staying away from Mack that she'd forgotten about the other Macholans in her life, the ones who had been her friends, her extended family.

"Aw, come on. It can be your wedding gift to me. Let me meddle in your love life."

Bailey fought to not roll her eyes. "You want to send me on a date as a wedding present for yourself?"

"Of course?" Jenna said emphatically. "It's better than getting a toaster."

Unable to help it, Bailey burst out laughing.

"What's so funny?" A deep, sexy voice came from behind her. She shivered and her stomach knotted in anxious excitement. Mack had found her.

"Oh, hey, Mack," Jenna said with a giggle, and suddenly she was holding up a sprig of mistletoe in their faces. "Oh dear, look at that, *mistletoe*," Jenna said in a tone of pretend shock and amazement.

Mack's cheeks actually turned pink, and Bailey's own face flushed with embarrassing heat.

"Hey, you have to do it, guys. Or it's bad luck," Jenna warned.

Mack shot Bailey a questioning look, and she tilted her head in silent invitation. *What the hell.* It wasn't as though this would be any worse than what they had done last night.

He cupped the back of her head and curled his other hand around her hip, the light but possessive hold sending shivers through her. Then he kissed her lightly, sweetly on the mouth.

"Son, that's not exactly a real kiss," Mack's father said, and they jerked apart in mortification.

"Yeah, Mack, don't wuss out," Jenna said. "Do it properly this time. It's not like she's your sister."

At this, Mack's eyes darkened as he gazed down at Bailey. "She's definitely not," he murmured before slowly leaning in again toward her as Bailey gave him an encouraging nod.

Bailey closed her eyes, trying not to think about their audience. Mack's mouth was on hers again, this time hot and demanding. Flashes of last night made her tremble against him, desperate to experience that all over again. She forgot anyone was watching. He parted her lips and slipped his tongue inside, reminding her of how incredible last night had been. She grabbed his shoulders, clinging to him. When they finally broke apart, she opened her eyes and glanced around. She and Mack were alone in the entryway. How long had they been kissing?

They both glanced around, and she exhaled a slow breath in relief that they were alone in the hall. Jenna and Mack's father had left them to finish that kiss privately. She and Mack stared at each other.

"We really need to talk," Mack murmured.

He held out his hand to her, and something caught in her chest as she put her hand in his. He curled his fingers around hers, leading her upstairs to his bedroom. Excitement fluttered in her belly as she realized she was once again the center of his attention.

It was strange, going into his room. The last time she'd been in his room, he'd been fifteen and she had been thirteen. He had shoved her into the hall after she'd gotten nosy and tried to open his nightstand drawer. He'd slammed his door, demanding privacy because he was a "man" and she was a kid. After that, she'd only seen the inside of his bedroom from her window when he had his blinds up. Now he led her into his sanctuary and closed the door, flipping the lock. She arched one brow in silent question.

"I think we can agree we both don't want anyone walking in on us."

That was true. Even if they were just talking, she didn't want anyone jumping to conclusions.

"So . . ." He still held her hand, and she only just realized it, but she didn't try to pull away.

"So . . . ," she echoed, strangely nervous to be alone with him while their families were downstairs. The muffled sounds of the party below were a reminder of what they were risking by sneaking away up here.

"I want more," Mack said softly.

"More?"

"More of this—more of *you*." He pulled her closer, his arms wrapping around her lower back. "Tell me I can have you for a few more days."

Bailey stared up into his mercurial eyes, full of winter storms. He slid one hand up her back until he held her head cradled in his palm. She leaned into his touch, and at the same moment her body tightened with anticipation.

"*Belong to me*, Bailey, for a little while longer." It was almost a command, and while she never bowed to a man for anything, when Mack spoke to her in that lust-roughened voice . . . her sanity went straight out the window.

"*Belong to me . . .*"

It was all she'd ever wanted, to belong to him. She was a fool no matter what she chose, so she might as well enjoy it.

"Yes," she breathed the single word that could throw her heart onto a fiery pyre, but at least she would go out with mind-blowing pleasure.

He didn't say another word, he simply kissed her hard, hungrily, insistently demanding entry to her mouth, and then she was spinning as he lifted her up and carried her toward his bed.

Mack was a lucky bastard, and he knew it. Bailey had granted him his Christmas wish. He sat back on his bed, and she straddled his lap. He slid his hands down her back, over her bottom, and up under the skirt of her plaid dress to cup her ass cheeks. His palm caressed the thin lace of her panties.

"You shouldn't have worn these," he murmured as he stole a slow kiss, using his tongue to remind her how much he enjoyed penetrating her in whatever way he could.

"Why?" She asked innocently, but rocked against his erection, rubbing herself on him.

"Because I want to rip them off and take you. Then you'd have to go back to your house and get another pair, naughty girl." He chuckled darkly. "Or maybe you want to spend the rest of the night bare so I can pull you away anytime and get what I want."

Her body shivered against his, and he fought off a groan as his blood surged to his groin. She brought out an animal side in him like no one else. She giggled, *actually* giggled, and the sound was so adorable that he laughed too. He had somehow forgotten what it was like to have Bailey in his life. He realized now more than ever that he didn't want to let her go again, so he would have to convince her to stay. And he was going to start with kisses.

He fisted his hand in her hair, relishing the way the golden-brown silk strands flowed over his palm. She ground down on his lap, and he groaned. Fuck, he needed inside her, bad.

"You're killing me, babe." He kissed her again, even rougher this time.

"Then punish me," she challenged and took his bottom lip between her teeth and tugged. The last thread of his control snapped. He rolled them over so she was on her back on the bed, but he got up and dug around in his drawer for a condom before coming back to her.

"On your knees," he ordered.

Bailey shot him a bratty pout and rolled over until she was kneeling on his bed with her back to him. She looked at him over her shoulder. He came up behind her and reached around her front and pushed his hand up between her thighs until he found her center and cupped it. He stroked his fingers over her mound through the thin lace of her panties. Her breath quickened as he pulled the lace aside and touched her wet, bare sex with his fingers.

Then he sank two fingers roughly inside her while he curled his other hand around her throat. He didn't squeeze at all—he simply held her prisoner, her back pressed to his chest while he pleasured her. Downstairs the house was full of guests, and no one knew what was happening in his childhood bedroom. He grew even harder at the thought of such tantalizing secrecy.

"Mack." Bailey gasped his name, and he moved his hand from her throat, covering her mouth while he ground against her body from behind. He continued to use his fingers to send her over the edge. He felt her clenching around his fingers. He rubbed the pad of one finger on her clit furiously until she was stifling her screams. Mack made her experience every hot second of her orgasm before he let her come down from the high of it. She sagged back against him, and he removed his hand from her mouth. She parted her lips, gasping in quick little inhalations. He held her close, curling himself around her as she trembled in his arms.

"What about you?" Bailey whispered and rubbed her ass against his groin. He was still hard as hell.

He wasn't sure what he planned to say, but then she turned on the bed and placed her hands on his chest, pushing him back a few steps and knelt on the carpet in front of him. She curled a finger in one of the belt loops of his jeans and tugged him a step closer. With the sultriest look he'd ever seen from any woman in his life, she unbuttoned his pants and unzipped his fly. Understanding now what she wanted, he freed his cock from his pants and stroked it as he gazed down at her. This was one fantasy he had denied himself, but now it was quickly becoming a reality. She leaned forward and flicked the tip of her tongue over the head of his shaft.

"Fuck," he moaned as she teased him. "Just take it all before you kill me." He was pretty sure he would agree to anything she asked for at this point if she did what her eyes promised she was about to do.

Her soft, husky laugh only made the blood pound harder in his ears. Bailey opened her mouth and took him inside. The feel of her wet mouth surrounding him made him nearly black out. He fought the urge to rock and fuck her mouth. He didn't want to scare her off when she was giving him one hell of a gift. She took him deeper and let him slide out before she smiled. A moment later, he lost all control and was tunneling in and out of her mouth, while she held on to his hips, her fingers digging into his flesh. She swallowed as he hit the back of her throat, and the exquisite sensation nearly made him come right then.

She hummed in delight as though she enjoyed it, and that was all it took. He thrust faster, and then he was coming apart at the seams. He tried to pull out, but she held fast, swallowing before releasing him.

Fucking hell, he was done for. That was it. She had wrecked him for all other women. She was a goddess, and he wanted to fall on his knees and worship her.

"Did . . . did I do it okay?" she asked. The sultry vixen was gone, and she was once again the sweet, smart, beautiful girl next door. He loved *the girl she'd been and now he loved the woman too.*

"Yeah . . . God, yes." He fixed his pants, and she climbed up off the floor with his help, and he pulled her against his chest. The need to cuddle her, to make her warm and happy with him, was overpowering.

"Good. I've never done that before," she admitted, her face reddening at the confession.

"You haven't?" She had just blown his circuits out, and that had been her first time?

"I've had a few boyfriends in the last couple of years, but I never really wanted to try that with them. But I wanted to try it with you." She tucked her face against his chest as though she was embarrassed.

"You're amazing. I . . . God, that was . . ." He had no words.

"I've struck you speechless," she said, chuckling to herself.

He could only manage a laugh in response to that.

Mack pulled her back onto his bed, and both of them stretched out lazily on it. She laid her head on his chest, and he stroked the shining waves of her hair. He didn't want to leave the cocoon of this room. He didn't want to give her up to the world again or let the festivities below separate them.

"You can see my bedroom from this angle," Bailey observed.

"Yeah." He didn't admit how many times he'd stared at her that year before he turned eighteen. She been so cute at sixteen, her long ponytail bouncing as she moved about her room. He'd always loved her energy—it made her glow. Everything around her seemed to be touched by that Bailey magic.

"You didn't ever watch me . . ."

"Undress?" he offered with a smirk.

"No, I mean . . ." She halted. "Yes, that's what I meant."

He rolled her beneath him on the bed so fast she didn't have time to fight him.

"What did you mean?" he asked. His gaze was locked on her mouth, that gorgeous mouth that had sent him to heaven only a few minutes ago.

"Nothing—"

"Bells," he growled softly. "Did I see you do what?"

She squeezed her eyes shut and wrinkled her nose as though fighting to keep her mouth shut. He leaned down and licked at the pursed seam of her lips, and she opened to him. He languidly teased her with slow kisses until she was pliant beneath him.

"Now spill it," he commanded in a seductive whisper.

"I used to . . . you know. I always watched you when you were in your room, and it made me flush so hot all over. I just couldn't help myself."

Is she saying . . . ? No, she can't be. "You got off watching me?" he asked.

She nodded slowly, her face as red as the elf costume she'd worn yesterday.

"I love knowing that." He grinned. It was so much more than a stroke to his ego. What he liked was knowing that she had discovered her sexuality while thinking about him. It felt special somehow.

"You're really okay with that? That I basically objectified you?"

He cupped her chin, raising her face to look at him. "You were thinking of *me*, right? Not just any sexy guy?"

"Right." She narrowed her eyes a little, as if trying to guess what he was going to say.

"Then I wasn't an object. You were seeing *me* in your fantasy." He brushed the backs of his knuckles over her cheek, marveling at how soft her skin was.

"Mack!" someone hollered up the stairs. It was his father's voice.

"Shit!" he whispered and slid off the bed and ran to the locked bedroom door. "Yeah, Dad?" he yelled through the closed door.

"What are you doing up there? Everyone's ready for dinner."

"I spilled something on my sweater. I'm changing." Mack opened his suitcase on the floor and dug through it, throwing clothes all about the room until he found a different sweater to wear. When he looked up, Bailey was sitting on the edge of his bed, swinging her legs with a grin.

"You'd better sneak down first. I'll change and follow you." He pulled his perfectly fine sweater off, and then she got up off the bed. She paused at his door and flicked the lock to open it. She bit her lip to hide a smile before she left. He changed into the dark gray Irish knit sweater. He saw that she'd left her lace panties on his floor. In that moment he knew he was forever in love with her. But what the hell was he going to do?

Seven

If anyone noticed that Bailey and Mack had been missing, they didn't show it. Luckily, Jenna's engagement was the primary focus of the night, and all the women were too busy oohing and aahing over the ring. The men were more concerned with college football bowl discussions. Mack breathed a sigh of relief that no one paid him or Bailey a second of thought during the entire dinner that the Macholan family hosted. He, Bailey, Rob, and Jenna ended up at the kids' table in the kitchen, while the adults sat in the dining room.

"Nothing ever changes," Mack chuckled as he stared at the two little children who shared the table with them. The kids belonged to one of his cousins, Tracy, who was ten years older than him. He had no idea what that made them, but they were Macholans, and that was enough to receive a warm welcome here.

"It's not too bad," Rob said, a pensive look on his face. "We can talk about *whatever* we want at this table."

"Like dinosaurs?" one of the little kids next to Mack asked. He couldn't have been more than six years old.

"Yes, *exactly* like dinosaurs." Rob smiled at the boy, and the two dove into a surprisingly heated debate about who would win a fight, a *T. rex* or a *Lythronax*. Mack couldn't miss the way Jenna was watching her fiancé and the child with adoration.

Oh boy . . . She had that starry-eyed look on her face that looked like his mother's whenever she reminded him that she wanted grandbabies someday. He turned his focus to Bailey, and she was watching the child too, a soft expression on her face. In that instant, he saw Bailey building a snowman with a red-cheeked cherubic child who had her eyes. The warmth in his chest blazed hot as he realized he wanted that for Bailey. No . . . he wanted that *with* Bailey.

He swallowed and quickly looked away. He caught Rob watching him, and Rob winked as though he read Mack's thoughts. Although he was uncomfortable that his thoughts were so transparent, he was glad to have someone like Rob joining the family. The guy was smart, funny, and thought Jenna was the answer to everything.

Which was exactly how a man who loved his favorite cousin should be.

Mack enjoyed sitting next to Bailey at dinner, their knees brushing beneath the cover of the table as the conversation flowed easily. It was as though Bailey had always belonged here with his family.

More than once, her honey-colored hazel-brown eyes would meet his gray ones as she said something, and her smile would brighten just a little, as though secretly for him, and damn him, he'd grin back at her like a fool. Then she'd brush one of her loose, curling locks of hair over her shoulder, and he'd get lost in the glossy ripples of her warm, walnut-colored hair. Everything about her was touchable, kissable, a tangible delight that he wanted to flood all his senses with.

He reached for her hand under the table, tracing his fingers over the back of her hand, and she turned her palm up toward his, their fingers sliding smoothly together and locking in a gentle hold.

As they finished their dinner, Mack was actually looking forward to the community theater's Christmas play. They abandoned the dishes on the counter, and everyone grabbed their coats. Carpools were arranged, and by a quirk of fate, he and Bailey ended up in his car, along with two of the kids, the little boy of six named Alex and a girl named Emma, who was about ten. Bailey made conversation easily with both kids. Mack was glad; he didn't spend much time with kids, but he liked them. Bailey was a natural.

He parked his car in the parking lot next to the theater, and their two young charges spotted their parents one car away and rushed over to them. Emma waved goodbye to Bailey, and that left Mack and Bailey alone on their walk to the theater.

"So . . . ," he began, trying to figure out how best to ask his question. "You like kids?" Well, so much for being subtle. Apparently, his mouth and brain weren't communicating well tonight.

"Yes." She laughed softly. "Why?"

"Oh . . ." He shrugged and pushed his hands into the pockets of his knee-length black coat. Then he crooked one elbow out toward her. She slipped her arm in his as if they'd done this a thousand times. The simple contact felt so right that every unsettled nerve inside him calmed with an infinite peace. "Do you want kids?"

She was silent a moment as they walked toward the glowing lights of the performing arts building. "I do. It doesn't have to be right away, but I do." She walked a few more steps before pausing. "Do *you* want kids, Mack?"

"I honestly never thought about it until tonight, but I do." He felt her relax next to him. They walked the rest of the way in companionable silence to the doors of the theater. The seating was open, and they chose seats in the middle where the sound would be the best.

The night felt strangely surreal to him as he removed his jacket and helped Bailey with hers and they settled in. It was completely natural to put his arm around her chair and then shift that arm to her shoulders. She moved, but toward him, not away. That ball of warmth in his chest spread a little more. The lights dimmed, and the red velvet curtains split on the stage to reveal a street in Victorian London.

"Marley was dead, to begin with," the narrator intoned dramatically as the actors filled the stage. Old man McGinty was dressed in a black suit and top hat as he prowled about the stage in a perfect miserly fashion befitting Ebenezer Scrooge.

As the story unfolded, Mack fell under its spell. The theme of the past, present, and future bound up by one's decisions hit too close to home. He found himself wondering what would have happened that night if he'd kissed Bailey before letting her go inside after the prom. What if he had seen her smile rather than cry? Would he have had ten years of her in his life? Would they now be married with a child or two sitting beside them in this very theater? To think that future had been erased all because he hadn't kissed her. A pang hit his heart so fiercely that he pulled Bailey an inch closer against him.

McGinty spoke in a clear voice, "I will honor Christmas in my heart, and try to keep it all the year. I will live in the past, the present, and the future." He faced the audience, beseeching them to believe him. Goosebumps broke out over Mack's arms, and he had the strangest feeling McGinty was speaking to *him*. As the play ended, neither he nor Bailey moved. They waited until most of the crowd cleared out before they stood to put their coats on.

"Oh, I see Jenna at the back." Bailey rushed to catch up with Jenna and Rob at the back of the theater, heading into the lobby. They stood talking and didn't seem to be in a rush to leave. Mack glanced back at the stage, as if drawn by something. He walked toward the little Victorian village setup. He climbed easily up on the stage and walked through the fake fallen snow on the stage. A little bit of it still trickled down from a snow machine above. The blue-and-white stage lights illuminated the white flakes as they drifted down past Mack's face.

"It's good to see you, Montgomery Macholan," a voice rumbled in a grandfatherly chuckle. Mack turned to find Mr. McGinty standing there. He had lost his Scrooge costume and was now dressed in a Santa costume. It was clear the man had plans tonight.

"Not heading home, Mr. McGinty?" Mack asked him. He was a little shocked to see that his grumpy old neighbor made a decent Santa.

"I visit the children's hospital every year, among other things." He adjusted the silver belt buckle on his pants.

His suit was far more real looking than the one Mack had worn for the company Christmas party.

"Wow, that's really nice of you."

The old man smiled. "I heard you were a good Santa for some special children this year."

Mack rubbed the back of his neck, embarrassed. "I did my best. It killed me that I couldn't help heal them. They're just kids. They deserve to have a full life ahead of them." The thought of those kids all having to face Christmas with uncertain futures made his chest tighten until it made it hard to breathe.

"All of life is us learning to *live*. Some are blessed with more time, and often they are the ones who realize their fortune the least." McGinty stroked his beard, and he fixed Mack with a meaningful look. "It's time you realized that *she's* your future. Stop wasting it."

Mack turned instinctively toward the doorway where he could see Bailey. When he looked back at McGinty, the man was already vanishing into the dark wings off the stage.

He stared at McGinty's back for a long moment before his eyes roved over the stage again, and a little chill rippled beneath his skin, making him feel strangely alive—and all the more determined to regain what he'd lost so many years ago. It was time to win Bailey's heart back and show her he would spend the rest of his life making her happy.

"Come on, Mack!" Jenna shouted at him, and he leapt off the stage and ran toward the doors, toward his future, toward Bailey.

Something was different about Mack tonight. Bailey lingered in the entryway of the Macholans' house long after everyone else had gone home.

"So what are you doing tomorrow?" Mack asked.

"What am I doing?" She laughed. "Christmas stuff. Cookies, presents, turkey, and all that kind of stuff."

He grinned almost bashfully. Who knew her charming boy next door was so wicked in bed and yet could still be bashful?

Tonight had been something out of a wonderful dream. Sharing dinner with his family and feeling like she fit in, holding his hand beneath the table, and walking into the theater on his arm. The little things dug into her heart, carving his name deeper in its walls. How his gray eyes had lit up as she'd shifted closer to him, and he'd curled an arm around her shoulders. They'd watched old McGinty play Scrooge, and that had been a kind of magic too in its own way, the timeless story of second chances spoke to her stronger than it ever had before. And now . . . now Christmas Eve was drawing to a close, and she didn't know what was to come next.

Mack shuffled his feet in the hall, and then his gray eyes, so electric met hers. "Let me see you tomorrow?" Something about that look, the storms brewing in his eyes and the way his golden hair was falling across his forehead . . . it brought back that night ten years ago, and her heart shuddered a painful few beats.

Bailey wanted to say yes, but for the first time that day her rational mind regained control and reminded her of everything she'd been through because of him.

"What are we doing, Mack?" Her good mood was fading away, and trying to catch hold of it was like trying to harness the wind.

Mack took her hands in his and was silent a long moment. The intensity of his gaze stunned her. She'd never had a man look at her like that before—like she was *everything.*

"I should have kissed you a long time ago, Bailey. Long before prom night. I was a fool. I've been a fool for a long time. These last two days have been a wake-up call. I walked away from you at the moment when I should have stayed, and that will *always* haunt me. Ten years I've lost. Ten years you could have been in my life." He smiled ruefully. "I guess what I'm saying is I'm done regretting things. I want you. I want you in my life." Mack's eyes glowed. "I want all of it with you. The wedding, the lazy Sunday mornings, the chaotic holidays with our families, dressing up as Santa for our kids."

Bailey's lips parted in shock. What was he saying? Was he asking her to marry him?

"Mack . . . I . . ." Her words quivered in the air, and he gave her hands a small squeeze.

"I know I'm springing this on you . . . Hell, I don't even have a ring. I've made a mess of this." He tried to laugh away his embarrassment.

"Time," Bailey said softly. "I need *time*, Mack." She pulled her hands from his. "You hurt me. You broke my heart, and I don't know if I can go through that again. You have to mean it, more than anything. You have to want me *forever*. If you got bored and just . . ." She didn't dare finish the thought.

"Bells." He reached for her, but she stepped back. If he touched her, she would lose her good sense and stay.

"I need to go. It's late." She started for the door, and her heart hammered as she heard his footsteps a second before she was spun around in his arms.

He cradled her close, his lips coming down on hers, but the kiss was infinitely tender, a soft, warm melding of lips. The kiss filled her head with visions of a long-ago night in his car when she'd leaned toward him, wanting everything from him and life. It was a kiss for a sixteen-year-old girl, the kiss she'd always dreamed of. She knew that no matter what happened tomorrow, the memory of this kiss would be the last thing she dreamed about every night. It would follow her wherever she went, a North

Star beckoning her home. When their lips parted, Mack held her face in his hands and touched his forehead to hers.

"I've loved you my entire life, Bailey Willis. There's never been anyone for me like you. It's always been you. I've just been too blind to see it." He nuzzled her cheek and then pressed a soft kiss to her forehead.

Bailey nearly opened her mouth, wanting to blurt out that she still loved him, would always love him, but she wasn't going to be that teenage girl again and let her heart get broken. She was too scared of the uncertain future with him to let him back in her life.

She closed her eyes, and then he stepped away, letting her go. His heat vanished as he pulled away, and she trembled as a cold far icier than the wind outside chilled her to her very bones.

Snow was falling outside as she crossed the space between their two childhood homes. She turned to look back. In the soft, snowy silence of Christmas Eve, she saw him framed in the doorway haloed by golden light. Snow swirled around in front of him as he watched her. For a moment, the flakes seemed to hum with all the words unspoken between them, before she couldn't bear it and rushed away.

Her mother and father had already gone to bed, and her house was quiet. She tiptoed up the stairs to her bedroom and closed the door. She leaned back against it and drew in a deep breath. Across the way, she saw Mack's bedroom light turn on. Her own room was dark, and she could watch him without being seen. He stood in his room, his hands shoved into his jeans pockets as he simply stared at the floor. Then he walked slowly over to his bed, sat down, and buried his face in his hands. He was so still, like he was frozen in a grief so great it had trapped him in a pillar of invisible ice. She knew that hunched, defeated pose more than anyone else. That was how she'd felt the night he'd broken her heart.

"Oh, Mack," she whispered. She wanted to believe him. That somehow he realized now, after all these years, that he loved her. But they were strangers with a shared childhood. That wasn't enough to risk her heart on.

She moved away from her bedroom door and sat down on her own bed, but she knocked something onto the floor. She heard the faint clink of metal. She leaned downward, her hand searching in the dark until she found whatever had fallen. It was the jingle bell Mack had bought her for Christmas so many years ago. She lifted it up, shaking it lightly, but no sound came out. Had she imagined the faint tinkle as it had fallen?

She placed the bell back in its box and put it on the nightstand. As her fingertips released the box, it gave a faint, solitary jingle. The silver of the bell was so bright it looked almost white in the pale moonlight coming in from her bedroom window.

Something inside her seemed to mend itself in that moment, and as she looked again toward Mack's window. She knew what she wanted. She pulled her cell phone out of her pocket and texted him one word.

Yes.

She held her breath as he tensed, and then he lowered his hands from his face and retrieved his cell phone from the bed beside him. He stared at the screen, and then his head turned her way. She reached for the lamp on her nightstand and clicked it on so he could see her. He rose from the bed and approached the window. She expected him to call her. Instead, he tapped something on his phone and then left the room, turning off the light.

What was he doing? Had she lost her chance?

Just as the panic and heartbreak threatened to swallow her, her cell phone buzzed with a text.

Wait there. Coming to you.

She continued to stare out her window, and a minute later, he emerged from the front door of his house. Mack was bundled up in his winter coat and snow boots. He headed toward the back side of his home. She could just see the edge of the Macholan backyard and his father's toolshed. Mack approached the shed and opened the door, disappearing briefly inside the darkness of it. When he emerged, he carried a ladder over one shoulder. Tramping through the snow, he marched up to her house with ease. He braced the ladder against the brick wall beneath her window.

It was then she realized what he was up to, and she opened her window, wincing as the frigid air blew into her face. She hastily tugged on the tabs to pop the screen off and let it fall into the snow beside the ladder. When she leaned over the window ledge, she saw Mack climbing up toward her. When he got to the top of the ladder, his face appeared in the center of her open window, and she knelt to be level with him. For a second they stared at each other, a brief uncertainty still sending nerves fluttering through her belly. His eyes were bright and burning like winter stars.

"Give me a second chance?" Mack asked, his voice a low whisper.

She nodded, reaching out to brush his hair from his eyes, and her fingers chilled with the dusting of snowflakes that clung to the golden strands. He leaned into the touch of her hand, and for a second she felt like Juliet when Romeo scaled the wall to her balcony. Mack could break her heart, but wasn't love worth the risk?

"Come inside before you freeze." She placed her hands on his own glove-covered ones. Then she moved out of the way, letting him crawl through the window. Mack closed it and turned to face her as he stood.

"Bells . . . ," he murmured, and she threw herself into his arms.

Mack held her so tight that she had trouble breathing at first. Then he let her go just long enough to throw his gloves off and shed his coat and snow boots. She backed up to the bed, and they toppled onto it together. She clutched at him, needing to feel him in her arms, to feel that this was happening, knowing what it meant. Mack's smile was soft in the moonlight as he stroked the backs of his fingers over her cheek.

"I missed you, Bailey. I missed everything about you, and all I want now is time with you, however long life gives us." His voice was low and rough with emotion, and Bailey's eyes burned.

"I missed you too, Mack. So much it hurts. You don't know what it's been like."

"I do, honey, I do. It's lonely. It's cold. It's like the North Pole without a hint of Santa Claus. It's no life at all, with nothing to believe in."

Tears escaped her eyes to roll down her cheeks, and he gently wiped them away.

"No, it isn't." She'd tried convincing herself for years that the time they were apart was full, complete, that there wasn't a gaping hole in her chest that had never healed. But the truth was, what she'd felt at sixteen for Mack, had never gone away. It wasn't a teenage infatuation. It was real. She'd found the mate to her soul so early in her life and had lost him too soon.

Mack kissed her cheek, then her forehead before finally kissing her mouth.

"I would give anything to go back to that night and kiss you . . . and never let you go. But if I did . . . if that was possible, I might never truly have learned how much you mean to me." He touched his forehead to hers, but this time he wasn't letting her go—he was holding on.

Pain and joy tugged her heart in two directions. The girl she had been would always remember that night and every lonely night that had followed. But the woman she had become felt a vast and infinite joy as powerful as the pain. Wasn't that life? To truly appreciate the joy by embracing the chance of sorrow as well?

"Promise me no more tears," Mack murmured. "I can't bear to see you cry."

She sniffled and tried to nod, but it was a promise she couldn't keep, and they both knew it.

"Perhaps I need to distract you." He peppered her face with kisses until she was giggling and writhing beneath him.

As she lost her breath he slowed, his hands sliding beneath her sweater. She wanted to be free of her clothes, and so did he. Despite their need, neither of them rushed this now. Clothes fell to the floor piece by agonizing piece, and only when they were skin to skin beneath the covers did they come together. Mack sank into her, and she threw her head back. Her only sounds were soft gasps and stifled moans as he filled her. The claiming was infinitely tender and infinitely perfect. This moment was about so much more than sex. It was about loving each other in every way they could. Making vows with their hearts, bodies, and souls.

Mack captured her hands against the bed on either side of her head and laced his fingers through hers, fusing them together. As excitement built in her body, everything around her seemed to intensify. The snowflakes falling in the moonlight outside were glittering fractals, and the feel of Mack's soft breath upon her face was comforting and exciting. His eyes were luminous in the dark, blazing for her alone. In his gaze she saw their future spiraling out ahead of her like a kaleidoscope with a thousand new dreams. All of them had Mack by her side.

"I love you, Bailey," he breathed. "I love all that you are, all that you will be."

She had no words left, only actions. She leaned up, her lips seeking his, kissing him with the fire of her love burning inside her and knowing he would taste that love upon her lips. Perhaps . . . perhaps Shakespeare did know a thing or two about love after all. When she came apart beneath Mack, the pleasure was so exquisite, so sharply perfect that she knew something inside her was changed forever. There was no going back. It was all or nothing with her and Mack.

"My God," he groaned and dropped his head to the

bedding beside her as they stayed fused together, their bodies a tangle of exhausted limbs. "Everything about that was magic," he murmured.

"What?" she whispered in exhausted confusion.

He slowly withdrew from her body and tucked her against him, pulling the covers tight around them.

"Magic . . . it's so deep within you . . . it's who you are." He smiled drowsily. "You're proof magic is real."

Bailey still didn't understand what he meant, but maybe she could puzzle it out in the morning.

"Stay with me?" She slid her arm around his waist beneath the covers, holding on to him.

"Always," he vowed.

Always . . . The word led her into a snowy world of dreams, with the Christmas dawn just hours away. Outside the snow continued to fall.

Eight

John Willis stepped off his front porch on Christmas morning and inhaled the fresh clean scent of snow in the air. There was no smell like it in the world. It was pure. That was the best way he could describe it. There was a purity of nature in snowfall. He walked down the driveway and then looked toward the Macholans' house. He noticed a set of footprints that led from the back of the neighbors' house toward the window below Bailey's room. A tall ladder leaned against the brick of his house, stopping just at the second-story window of his daughter's bedroom.

"Huh . . ." He walked over to the ladder and brushed the snow off its rungs. The name *Macholan* had been written along the flat part of the ladder in black marker.

He moved his gaze between Bailey's window and the window that faced hers in the Macholans' house. Mack's room.

With a slow smile, he chuckled and shook his head.

"About damned time." He picked up the ladder and carried it toward Mike Macholan's backyard shed, whistling as he did so.

Mack woke slowly, as though the pleasant dreams he'd had all night held him gently in that place between waking and dreaming. Snow-white light illuminated Bailey's bedroom. As he gazed down at the top of her head, which was pillowed on his chest, he was overcome by that same overwhelming, unbearable joy. Maybe it was possible to die from happiness. He wasn't used to this level of euphoria, but he welcomed it openly. He stroked a hand over the strands of her brown hair, which held a golden tint in the morning light. She stayed wrapped around him, cuddling against him like he was a treasured stuffed animal. For some reason, the thought made him smile. He liked being Bailey's favorite toy. Oh yes, he would be *anything* she wanted him to be.

When she finally stirred from sleep, she yawned and then froze, as if reality had just dawned and she suddenly realized where she was and who she was wrapped around.

"Mack." Her sleep-softened voice and those beautiful hazel-brown eyes fixed on his face, and his heart hammered wildly. He really had been blind to live next to her their entire childhood and never see her for who she really was. His future. His beginning, his end, his everything in between.

"No regrets about last night?" she asked, worry darkening her face.

"Only that I didn't come to you sooner."

Relief illuminated her soft hazel-brown eyes, and she let out a soft breath that warmed his skin.

"Let's not talk about what we should have done. Let's think instead of what we *will* do," Bailey said as she scooted up his body a few inches and straddled him. Mack groaned as she rubbed her naked body against his.

"I loved last night," Bailey said as she tiptoed her fingers up his chest. "But promise me that bad boy Mack will always be there when I want him." She let the covers drop to her waist and arched her back. Her breasts, so perfect, taunted him.

He sat up and wrapped one arm around her back as he leaned in and took one nipple into his mouth, sucking hard. She clutched the back of his head, digging her fingers into his hair and whimpering softly as he lightly bit her nipple. Then he kissed a path to her other breast, and she wriggled as he slid one palm under the sheet and smacked her plump little ass. God, he was going to enact so many fantasies about her ass.

"You want bad Mack?" He fisted a hand in her hair, and then before she could answer, he kissed her hard and hungry. He didn't let her have a moment to breathe until he was satisfied with his kiss. Then he lifted her off his lap and growled softly, "On your hands and knees, babe."

She complied, and he knelt behind her on the bed, one hand curled around her hip. His other hand fisted his cock as he guided himself into her.

"Fuck, you're so tight." He saw stars as he thrust inside her. She squeezed him, the wet, hot feel of her too perfect to be real. He slid his hand around her thigh to find her mound. Then he stroked her until he found the little bud of her clit. She jolted and gave a little half gasp, half squeak, and he chuckled. He wasn't going to let her come until he was certain he would overwhelm her. He wanted her to remember this Christmas morning for the rest of their lives.

He withdrew and slammed back into her, working her into a frenzy. She dropped her face into the pillows in an attempt to muffle her sounds as he pounded against her ass. God, he'd never felt this connected to anyone during sex. It was like he and Bailey fit more than just physically. The pleasure this gave him wasn't just physical. So much more of it was emotional now.

Mack lifted her up so they were both on their knees,

and then he turned her face to the side and claimed her mouth with a hot kiss as he rammed his hips faster and faster against her backside. When he stroked her clit again, she cried out against his mouth. He swallowed her scream of pleasure and then released himself inside her. It was only when they collapsed on the bed that he remembered a condom and the fact that he *hadn't* used one.

"Bailey . . ." He closed his eyes. "Sorry, I forgot to use a condom."

She pressed a kiss to his jaw. "I'm on birth control. It's okay."

He let out a breath of relief, then realized how bad that might seem. He cupped her face. "For the record, I'm all in for kids. I just want you to be ready too. We should have a year to travel and enjoy being married before we add to the Macholan clan."

"You mean the *Willis* clan," Bailey corrected with a rebellious laugh.

"The Willis *hyphen* Macholan clan," he compromised, emphasizing their joined names.

"Perfect." Bailey kissed him. It was a soft, lingering kiss that was full of love, so much love his heart quivered in his chest.

"I love you," he whispered when their mouths parted.

"I love you too." She bit her lip shyly, and he pulled her even closer to him.

"Let's stay in bed all day."

"Our parents might object to that," she giggled.

"Fine." He stroked a fingertip down her beautiful nose and then traced her lips. "We eat turkey, open presents, then go to bed, and then we eat cookies and then go to bed again."

"Bailey! Come down for breakfast," her mother shouted from the bottom of the stairs.

"Shit. I better escape out the window." Mack gave her one more kiss before he got out of bed and began pulling his clothes on. When he finished pulling on his jeans, he paused by the window. "What the hell?"

"What is it?" Bailey sat up, clutching the sheet to keep herself warm and covered.

"My ladder's gone."

"You're kidding." Bailey flopped back on the bed. "I guess someone knows you're in here, then."

"One of our dads, that's for sure," Mack muttered, and then when he turned back he bumped the nightstand and something hit the floor, making a clear, crisp jingling sound. He bent to pick it up. It was a large silver bell. He gave it a little shake and grinned at the stunned expression on Bailey's face.

"Yours?"

"Yeah . . . the one you gave me for Christmas when I was twelve. It stopped working. It used to ring."

Mack stared at the bell in his palm. The silver was so

bright that it seemed almost white. He swallowed hard as a strange emotion he couldn't name took hold of his chest.

"Bailey, the one I gave you all those years ago was broken from the start." He shook the bell, hearing the crisp, clear jingle. This one was definitely not broken.

"Last night, when I thought we would never . . ." Bailey swallowed hard. "It wouldn't ring. It was silent."

He understood what she meant. A bell that didn't ring, a silence that seemed more silent than imaginable. It was a silence of the heart, one that you felt, not just heard. It was why he'd called Bailey "Bells." Because for him, she'd always been the ringing sound of a Christmas jingle bell. A beautiful sound that filled him with love and hope. He'd almost forgotten that...until he heard *this* bell ring.

He shook the bell again, that beautiful sound filling the air as though everyone on earth could hear it. A broken bell that was no longer broken . . . a bell that rang into the bright, endless Christmas morning. Bailey's eyes were wide and full of questioning wonder as she stared between him and the bell.

It was then that Mack realized he *believed*.

Mr. McGinty sat on a wooden park bench that faced the rows of houses on the street where he'd lived the last twenty-eight years. He held his cane, his black leather gloves trimmed with white ermine fur. He blinked away the falling snowflakes that clung to his lashes. It was another perfect Christmas. Now it was time to move on, time to find the next place that needed a little more magic.

He slowly rose from the bench, his eyes still on the Willises' house as he heard the clear sound of a jingle bell ringing. His smile grew and he let out a deep belly laugh of pure joy that echoed in the air.

"It only took you twenty-eight years to *believe* in me, Mack."

Only the snowflakes witnessed the twinkle in Mr. McGinty's eyes as he vanished into the beautiful snowy Christmas morning.

Thank you so much for reading *Stocking Stuffer*! If you want to warm up with a steamy enemies to lovers summer romance, turn the page to read the first 3 chapters of *Summer Heat Wave*!

Summer Heat Wave

PROLOGUE

Paradise Island, the Bahamas

The waves came rushing along the debris-strewn beach toward Blair Ashworth as the hurricane winds nearly knocked her down. Palm trees bent and whipped beneath the onslaught of the storm. The once pure blue sea was black, and the sand was cold and wet as it dragged her feet down in terrifying suction. Fear seized her heart in its claws, squeezing until she could barely breathe, as another wave surged toward her. They hadn't seen the storm coming, not this fast . . .

Water knocked her off her feet, and she fell, her hands hitting concrete as she collided with the resort sidewalk. Strong arms grasped her body, lifting her up and bracing her against a wall of hot, determined male. The intense warmth she felt had nothing to do with the current danger of the storm and everything to do with the man who'd just saved her. A man who *shouldn't* have saved her because he despised her.

"Can you walk?" Denver Ramsey's deep voice rang out crisply across the howling wind, stilling her panic and the rush of chaotic thoughts in her head. His voice demanded that she respond, that she meet the challenge of being brave.

"Y-yes . . . I think so." Blair ignored the stab of pain in her knees and forearms. They had to keep moving and get to safety or risk being pulled out to sea by the next wave.

"Let me help you." An arm gripped her waist, holding her close to the hard male body it belonged to. She lifted her head to stare into the devastatingly perfect face of Denver Ramsey. The man she had been sent to seduce . . . into a business deal. A man who hated her with every breath in his body.

Yet here he was, saving her life as a storm ravaged the beautiful island he called home. Wind whipped his dark hair into his hazel eyes, which looked darker as they reflected the stormy skies above them. His once crisp white dress shirt soaked with the rain and surging seawater, clung to his muscled form.

"Just a bit farther," Denver assured her as they trudged down the walkway toward the entrance to the private luxury apartments of the Seven Seas Beach Club. Water swamped the sidewalk, and he held her closer, keeping her on her feet when she might have been knocked down again. The doors opened, and two resort employees in raingear rushed out to help them.

"Are you all right, sir?" one of the men asked Denver as he handed him a small towel.

"Yes, thank you. Are all of the guests safe?"

"Yes, sir. All safe and accounted for. We have implemented the hurricane protection plan. All of the housing is secure as well. The National Weather Service has already downgraded the storm to a category one, and within a few hours we should have clear skies again."

Denver still held Blair close, but she shivered as a chill from the icy ocean settled in her bones. Now aware of her shaking, he looked down at her, and without words he used the towel to dry her face and as much of her as he could manage before the towel was soaked.

"Miss Ashworth and I will be in my apartment. Call me if you need me." He handed the towel back to the employee.

"Yes, sir." The employee returned to the front desk.

Blair followed Denver through a hallway decorated with stunning seascapes portraying the many faces of the ocean, from gentle surf to raging waves. Just like everything at the Seven Seas, they were top quality, elegant, and like the club's owner, the pieces also held a bit of mystery.

Denver released his hold on her waist and lifted his

right wrist, which bore a silver metal band. He waved the band in front of the electronic door lock, and it clicked open. Then he opened the door and stepped aside, allowing her to enter.

It was a bad idea to go anywhere alone with him, though not because he was dangerous. He *was* dangerous, but not in a way that threatened her. Rather, Denver Ramsey was dangerous to any woman who wanted to keep her head on straight, her heart safe, and her panties on. On his good days, the man looked like a tempting water god, but right then he looked like a vengeful Poseidon. She inwardly flinched, knowing just how deep his dislike of her ran. Hell, one could almost call his cold disdain for her *hate*. But Denver didn't know her well enough to truly hate her. No, his true hate was reserved for her father and her uncle.

Once she was inside his apartment, he closed the door with a frightening finality. He nodded toward a room beyond her, and she turned to find a wide, open sitting room with thick glass doors that revealed a stunning view of the stormy sea.

"Sit down," he ordered, though his tone was softer than she expected.

Blair collapsed onto the nearest armchair and winced at the feel of her wet clothes on the expensive blue-and-white-striped fabric.

He disappeared down a hall and returned with two

fluffy white bath towels and a first aid kit. He quickly dragged a towel over himself before tossing it on the surface of the coffee table. Then he handed the second one to her. She accepted it and wiped her face, her hair, and her clothes, which were hopelessly ruined. The navy-blue sundress with white polka dots and her cork wedge sandals had been a great choice three hours ago, long before she'd known this tropical storm would sweep their way so quickly.

Denver set the first aid kit on the table and pulled another armchair toward her before sitting in it.

"Let me see your knees." He gestured at her skirt, and she lifted the wet fabric up just past her knees. Bloody scratches covered her knees and her forearms. He opened the kit and removed several antiseptic wipes. He wiped at the wounds, and she bit her lip, hiding her reaction to the sting of the antiseptic.

"Where were you going? Didn't you hear the storm siren?" he asked, his voice still dangerously soft. He didn't look at her as he cleaned her cuts and bandaged them. Then he gestured for her arms, which he saw to next.

"I was out scouting for the best location to do photos for the adjustments on the campaign."

"It isn't worth dying over." At her gasp, he lifted his gaze to hers, his hazel eyes burning hot.

"It could be, since my job depends on it," she muttered.

"I haven't even agreed to work with you," he reminded her. "Our bargain only included that I would give it my honest consideration."

"That's because you haven't heard my pitch—" she started.

"Not a chance," Denver snapped, cutting her off. Then his voice gentled. "There's nothing you could show me that could change my mind." His scowl shouldn't have made him even more attractive, but it gave her the most wicked fantasies of what he'd do to her ass while he wore that scowl.

"Nothing?" A pit formed in her stomach. Blair had been so convinced that she could win him over. The ad campaign she and her team had worked up in the last week was more than solid. It was damn brilliant. Especially now that she'd come here and added her final touches after seeing the magic of his resort and the island through his eyes.

"There's only one thing I told you I truly want from you, and we both know that would be a terrible idea." He was still facing her, his knees almost touching hers as his gaze held hers.

"Terrible," Blair agreed breathlessly as his focus moved to her mouth. She couldn't stop staring at his lips.

He reached up to cup the back of her neck. His hand was warm, large, and wonderful as he held her neck in a gentle but dominating hold.

"Then again, maybe this one little mistake won't change anything," he mused.

Blair's heart pounded, ramming against her ribs like the waves outside battered the shore. There was nothing worse than wanting something—someone—she shouldn't, but she still wanted Denver Ramsey's kiss more than anything in that moment.

Denver closed the distance and captured her lips with his in piratical perfection, like a man who knew he'd conquered her and won. She hated him and loved him for it.

Yes, it was a terrible mistake, and it would change *everything*.

Chapter 1

Chicago
One week earlier

"Blair, Randall wants to see you." Kayley leaned into Blair's cubicle.

"He does?" Blair immediately tried to quell a flurry of nerves. Even though she had known Randall Ashworth her whole life—he was her uncle, after all—she had never been comfortable around him. He had an underlying meanness to him that made her uneasy.

"Yeah, he said you should come quick or he would give the new account opportunity to one of his account executives." Kayley West, who was one of Blair's closest friends, always had her back.

"Thanks, Kayley."

"No problem." Kayley stepped back to let Blair past her as she exited her cubicle. "I'm grabbing Hackney's for lunch. You want to share a soup-and-sandwich combo?"

"Sure, thanks." Blair smoothed her black pencil skirt and tweaked her teal blouse into place before making the dreaded walk down the length of cubicles to her uncle's corner office. His door was closed, so she rapped her knuckles on the thick wood and held her breath.

"Come in," Randall barked.

Blair opened the door and found her uncle seated at his desk, his laptop open. He didn't look up when she entered.

"Close the door behind you."

She followed his command and stood, rather than sat. She knew better than to sit until this man invited her to.

Randall Ashworth was a tall, lean man who bore only a passing resemblance to her father, his younger brother. Where her father's face was lit with warmth, Randall's was cold, his lips thin and his brows severe. Blair had seen pictures of the brothers as young men, and both Paul, her father, and Randall had been dashing. But her father had kept his good looks longer than Randall. Blair was convinced that her uncle's greediness had played a role in the way his looks had hardened into such severity.

"Sit down, Blair." He waved at the pair of black leather armchairs facing his desk.

Blair perched on the edge of one, keeping silent.

"I know you are interested in moving up to an account executive position and leaving the art department."

"Yes." Blair kept her tone neutral. Her uncle wasn't above dangling an opportunity and then yanking it out of reach when he sensed she wanted it too much. Ever since he had forced her father into early retirement fifteen years ago through a cheap buyout of his half of the company stock, her uncle had only Blair to kick around when he wanted to indulge in family pettiness.

"Well, I am offering you the position if you bring a specific client in for a five-year contract." He announced it offhandedly, as though he didn't even care.

"Who's the client?" Blair asked.

"The Seven Seas Beach Club on Paradise Island in the Bahamas." He didn't even pause in examining whatever he was looking at on his computer.

Blair's heart skipped a painful beat. "Randall, that's one of Denver Ramsey's companies, isn't it?"

Her uncle continued to study his laptop screen. "It is."

"But—"

"Do you want the account executive position?"

"Of course I do," she answered carefully, desperately searching for the right language that would mollify him and broach the real problem at hand. "But you know we would be the last company that he would take a pitch from, let alone sign with. I would be escorted from his property by security."

Her uncle was crazy for thinking that Denver Ramsey would let her near his accounts, not after what had happened between their fathers more than fifteen years ago.

"Blair, if you can land the Seven Seas account for five years with no termination options, I will sell you your father's partnership interest at a tenth of the appraised market value." His deep voice was almost oily, slickly sliding into her head and pulling out the one thing that could make her risk everything.

Hearing that, the dozens of protests rambling through her head simply vanished. She could get her father's share of Bay Breeze Creative Solutions back. Her throat constricted slightly. That had been her dream, her true goal for the last five years when she'd first started working here—to earn back what her father had been forced to give up.

"Well?" Her uncle sat back in his chair, his dark-brown eyes almost a pair of obsidian pools that showed no emotion.

"Can I have until the end of the day to think about it?"

She saw the briefest flash of triumph in his eyes. "You have one hour."

Blair got to her feet and left her uncle's office. She returned to her cubicle and nearly collapsed in her seat.

Could she do it? Could she find some way to convince Denver Ramsey that he should hire her for his advertising campaign? What could she possibly say to him that would change the past?

Blair turned on her laptop and searched for Denver Ramsey on the internet. She hadn't kept tabs on him since her father had left the company fifteen years ago. Of course, when that had happened, she'd been only thirteen years old. All she remembered from back then was her mother crying a lot, and that her father had barely survived the shame of what he'd done to the Ramseys. Somehow, her damn uncle had coasted through it all without even a blemish. Life really wasn't fair.

The moment she hit *search*, the screen filled with a dozen articles and photos, all featuring a tall, dark-haired god of a man who wore his suit in a way that made a woman clench her thighs together. She clicked on the *Vanity Fair* article from two years ago. The main photo in the article showed Denver wearing trousers and a white shirt that was halfway buttoned up as he leaned against the trunk of a palm tree. The azure sea and white sand created a tropical backdrop. The man was painfully beautiful.

The title of the article read, "Wonder of the World, a True Paradise Escape." The article went on to describe

Denver's meteoric rise in private equity and his transition to the development of one of the most exclusive island resorts in the world. All starting at the age of twenty-three.

"Wow . . . Who is that? He looks familiar," Kayley asked as she popped into Blair's cubicle and sat in the spare chair that Blair kept for her.

"That's Denver Ramsey." Blair sighed as a headache began to pound behind her eyes.

"He is seriously hot as hell. Do you know him?"

"Me?" Blair shook her head. No, she had never met him. But she remembered him. It was hard to forget the picture of a seventeen-year-old boy standing by the grave of his father, who had died after losing his business because of *her* father. That image was burned into her brain for the rest of her life.

"Wait, scroll down. I want to read that." Kayley scooted her chair closer. "He lost his dad at seventeen and had to leave high school to work full-time to support his mother."

A ringing started in Blair's ears, piercing her skull like a distant train whistle. Kayley kept reading aloud.

"He got his GED and got into Princeton on a full scholarship and worked part-time while still achieving a double major. Holy shit."

Kayley had had no idea. Denver had persevered and prospered after the great tragedy of losing his father and his home. He had built an empire all his own. If Blair hadn't felt sick at the thought of her father's part in Denver's adversity, she would have been honored and anxious to meet such a man and do business with him.

"Wait, Blair . . ." Kayley's voice softened as she pointed to a few lines in the article. "That's your dad's old company, isn't it? The one that later became this company?"

Blair silently read the few lines Kayley pointed to:

Despite the unethical practices by Bay Water Ad Agency that led to Mr. Ramsey's father's advertising agency being closed and investigated for wire and mail fraud and eventually his death, Mr. Ramsey has weathered the death of his father and created a fortune all his own—one above reproach.

There was a quote from Denver in bold below that.

"My father was later cleared by the FBI, but by then the damage was done. He died from the stress and trauma of the investigation. I would give anything to go back in time and tell him to stay calm—that it would soon be over and he would be proven innocent—but we can't go back, no matter how much we might want to." The quote was accompanied by a moving profile shot of Denver sitting in the sand, his legs bent up and his arms resting on his knees as he gazed at the surf and the setting sun.

"What happened?" Kayley whispered.

"It's a long, awful story, but my dad made a mistake, one that cost him a lot." Blair didn't want to talk about that. Her father hadn't died like Denver's, but he had suffered greatly for the mistake he had made by accusing Denver's father of those crimes.

"So . . . Why are you looking at him?" Kayley asked. "I sense this isn't some rosy walk down memory lane."

Blair closed her eyes and rubbed her temples. "Randall offered me an account executive position and fifty percent of the company if I can get Ramsey to sign a binding five-year ad contract with us."

"Oh my God," Kayley gasped. "Are you going to do it?"

"It's impossible. There's no way he'd even agree to meet with me." Blair opened her eyes and stared at the screen again, at the almost savage beauty of Denver Ramsey and the sea beyond him. He stood on the path to her dream, to owning half the agency her father had built. If she could get fifty percent under her control, she'd only have to wait for her uncle to retire and then she would achieve her dream of running her own agency.

"Blair, you have what it takes. You're an amazing art director. You have an incredible vision for campaigns. Prepare one and then wow him. He would have to be insane not to want to work with you after you show him how capable you are at your job, family issues aside. It's worth a shot. If you don't try, you'll never know what might've happened, right?"

As always, her friend was right.

"Okay, but I'll need your help. I want to get down there in a week with a decent pitch."

"Wait, are you going to go to the Bahamas?" Kayley sighed. "I hate you." Then she hugged Blair. "Seriously, we'll lock this in, and you'll get the promotion and your share of the company."

"I do not deserve a friend like you." Blair hugged her back.

"Just remember that when you're on some beach basking in the glory of the signed contract."

"I will," Blair promised with a chuckle.

She opened her email account and sent a message to her uncle: *I'll do it.*

Denver Ramsey arched his body, dove through the cresting wave, and plunged into a world of brilliant blue water. The midday sun hit the frothing surface and scattered its beams into ripples of light that illuminated the coral reef just past the break line of the waves. He moved his arms in gentle strokes, pushing his way farther from shore as he studied the aquatic world beneath him.

A peacock flounder coasted along the ocean floor, blending in almost seamlessly with the surrounding sand. A small octopus sprang off a nearby rock and drifted past him. He reached out and brushed his fingers over the trailing tentacles, and the octopus curled around his wrist, playfully exploring him with its small suckers before letting go and coasting back to the seafloor. A pair of bright yellow-and-green queen angelfish floated gracefully past him, completely undisturbed by human intrusion into their world.

The ocean gave him such a sense of peace, one that he desperately needed. Even after all these years, Denver fought to keep the pain of the past and his responding anger under control. The sea had become his haven. Even though it was seemingly ever-changing, there was still a beautiful permanence to it that grounded him.

He swam for another half hour over the reefs before riding the waves back to shore. The strip of beach where he surfaced was part of the Seven Seas Beach Club's private property. Small grass huts dotted the beach a ways back from the waves, where they stayed clear of the tides. The guests of his resort lounged on beach chairs and on waterproof canopy beds shielded from the sun by adjustable sunshades. The resort restricted occupancy levels so the beaches weren't crowded.

Denver collected his cell phone and towel from one of the chairs and dried off his body before he checked his phone. His operations manager, Simon Wells, had left him a few text messages with polite but urgent requests to call him back.

He dialed Simon's number and tossed his towel on the

beach chair while he combed his fingers through his wet hair to get it out of his eyes.

"Simon," he said the second his operations manager answered.

"We just heard from the Fawkes Group. The owners, Jack and Anne Hudson, are coming next week to see you about your Bali resort proposal."

A thrill of triumph surged through Denver. He'd had his eye on this deal for more than a year, but he needed a good investment group interested in exclusive resorts to back him. He wanted to re-create the magic of the Seven Seas Beach Club with his new idea. Atlantis Rising would be built on the coast of Bali by next year if he stayed on track.

"That's great news. You'll make all the arrangements?"

"Yes, but we have a slight hitch." Simon cleared his throat.

"Hitch?"

"Yes. Jack Hudson wants you to call him. I've texted you his private cell number. He said he had a few questions he wanted to ask you."

"Questions?" Denver repeated in a flat tone. "What kind of questions?"

"I have no idea," Simon rushed to answer.

"I'll handle it. Thanks, Simon." Denver hung up, and a moment later Hudson's cell number came through in a text. Denver dialed the number and waited. After two rings, Hudson answered.

"This is Jack."

"Jack, this is Denver Ramsey. Simon Wells, my operations manager, said you had a few questions for me?" He eased down onto the beach chair and watched the light play on the surface of the ocean while he waited for Hudson to speak.

"Denver, glad we got connected. I guess Wells told you we plan to come out and visit next week?"

"He did."

"Well, you know that my company is built on family relationships. My wife is my business partner. I've asked around about you, and everyone has the best things to say . . . but, well, the rumor is you can be ruthless in business. I used to be ruthless before I found Anne, but being in love, marrying her, it made me a better man and an even better businessman. I suppose what I'm asking is rather personal, but there's no nice way to say it. Are you planning on settling down? My wife and I would feel more comfortable knowing we are evenly paired in this deal for the Bali resort with a man who understands teamwork and relationships."

Denver's grip tightened on his phone as he sensed the danger of losing out on the investment. It was ridiculous. Being a damn bachelor should've been an advantage, not a liability.

"I keep my personal life rather private," he hedged as he ran through a dozen scenarios of what to say. His gaze settled on a pair of women who passed by him, both shooting coy smiles his way. An idea leapt into his mind.

"I do have a serious girlfriend, Jack. But I have kept it quiet. In fact, I was planning to propose to her this week."

"Oh? We hadn't heard—" Hudson began.

"Like I said, I keep my life private. After what happened to my father, you can't blame me."

"That's true. I'm sorry I asked. It's important to us, that's all. I really need to know you're a team player, in for the long haul. A good relationship can show that."

"Yeah." Denver couldn't believe it. He had to find a woman he could talk into posing as his girlfriend, pull off a quick proposal, and then keep up the pretense until contracts were signed. After that, he and his "fiancée" could have a change of heart.

"Well, it's settled, then. We'll be on Paradise Island next week. I'll have my assistant send you our travel information once we have it."

"Wonderful," Denver replied, putting all the false cheer that he could muster into the word. Thankfully, Hudson didn't seem to notice. The moment the call ended, Denver threw his phone onto his towel and stifled a groan.

He needed to find a fake fiancée, and fast.

Chapter 2

Five days later

Blair stepped off the small shuttle bus once it parked in front of the main lodge at the Seven Seas Beach Club, and her eyes widened. The resort was even more spectacular than the pictures on the website. She'd studied Seven Seas extensively as part of her research for her campaign before she'd left Chicago. The entire complex had a loose but logical layout, with the main lodge in the center, which housed a massive dining hall, reception room, lobby, and corporate offices as a central hub. The apartments and suites were arranged in separate buildings expanding outward like the arms of a starfish. It left her with the relaxed feeling of being able to walk everywhere but not being too far away from anything.

"Welcome to the Seven Seas!" The young man left the valet station and met her by the shuttle.

"Thank you." She stepped aside to allow the other guests to exit the vehicle.

"What's the name on your reservation?" The man pulled out a slender tablet and opened up the active reservation list.

"Blair Ashworth."

"Oh, yes, the Siren bungalow in the Nautilus complex. Let's get you all signed in, and then we'll have someone sit with you and explain the resort's layout and amenities before taking you to your lodgings."

She followed the man into the lobby. It was a grand circular room with white marble floors. Blue tile mosaics enhanced with brilliant gold and silver accented the lobby walls, and the domed ceiling was painted with detailed marine life. Sunlight poured through the atrium, making everything glow softly. After she checked in, she was given a silver wristband containing a waterproof chip.

"You just hold up your wristband to the black pad on your door, and it will open up. It will activate the safe in your closet as well."

Blair studied the fancy wristband. It had to be expensive, but it was genius. Keycards got lost too easily.

"You can also upload funds into your account and use

your wristband to pay for anything at the resort. Now, if you'll follow me, I'll get you a map and an escort to the Nautilus complex." The man handed her a glossy foldable map and had a golf cart brought around. She and her luggage were loaded up, and the young woman in khaki shorts and a pale-blue polo shirt grinned at her from the driver's seat.

"Nautilus?" the woman asked.

"Yep." Blair sat in the passenger seat of the golf cart, and then it shot forward. They cruised down a gravel path beneath the palm trees.

"I'm Erica. Is this your first time here?" the driver asked.

"Yes, both at the resort and in the Bahamas. It's so beautiful here."

Erica chuckled. "Island living either draws a person in completely or it doesn't attract them whatsoever. You love it or you hate it. I came here for spring break at age twenty and fell in love. I went back to college and switched my major to hospitality and hotel management. Then I graduated, got a job here, and haven't left since except to go home to see my family on holidays."

"Really? What about island life attracts you?" Blair asked. Erica was the perfect person to talk to for inspiration for Blair's pitch to Denver Ramsey.

"I guess it's that I feel closer to nature. There is a peace here that is hard to explain. Even though there are wild storms sometimes, you still feel restful here. The pace of life is slower, your stress lower. And the beauty—all the blues, golds, yellows, and whites," Erica added thoughtfully. "Cheery but peaceful colors."

"I noticed the hotel has a color scheme that's limited, carefully thought out, well designed and consistent."

Erica nodded as she took a turn in the cart, driving down another pathway. "The hotel owner had an active hand in the design. He didn't leave a single detail out when he created this place. Every apartment has its own theme, and the overall resort was built with an intense dedication to the ocean, so the fantasy of the sea is unparalleled."

"Could you give me an example of that?"

Erica checked her watch as she stopped in front of a series of close-set bungalows. A large sign with a nautilus shell indicated they had reached the right place.

"Be sure to schedule a dinner reservation near the aquarium at seven tonight and you'll see. It's worth it."

Blair made a mental note.

"You're in Siren, so that's the first one here. You remember the way we came?" Erica lifted her suitcase from the golf cart.

"Yeah," Blair assured her.

"Excellent. Well, if you need anything, call the front desk or dial zero." With a wave, Erica headed back up the path in the golf cart, and Blair turned toward the bungalow. It was a three-room suite with a master bath and a cozy porch that faced the sea. The view was worth every penny. The privately owned beach restricted access to it, which meant only a handful of grass huts and chairs dotted the white sandy shore a quarter of a mile from her bungalow.

Blair lifted her suitcase up the three steps to the porch and activated her door lock with her wristband. Then she rolled her suitcase deeper inside and left it by the bedroom so she could admire the suite.

Sea-blue walls with white trim and classy mermaid-accented decoration pieces made Blair feel like she was fully immersed in a seascape. The white wooden book-shelves and dining room table were covered with various shells, from large conch shells to flat silver dollars. She picked up one of the larger shells, her fingertips coasting along the soft-pink inner surface of the shell's opening. Then she placed the shell back down and explored the rest of the rooms before she came back for her suitcase. Before she started on work, she wanted to take an hour to soak up some rays on the beach.

She changed into a modest two-piece swimsuit. The bright red color looked good with her long brown hair, which she tied back to keep it from getting hopelessly windblown. Then she grabbed her sunglasses, hat, sandals, and a towel.

The walk to the beach was pleasant, and by the time

she got to the white sand and slipped off her sandals, that sense of peace Erica had talked about had settled over Blair. She wriggled her toes in the pale, warm grains and let out a relaxed sigh. A light breeze cooled her skin and rippled through the fronds of the nearby palm trees. As much as she was enjoying herself, she was also making mental notes about the atmosphere of the resort property, as well as the influence of nature. Later this week, she would take some photos to add to her pitch, assuming Denver didn't feed her to the sharks before then. The thought of Denver and his inevitable anger encroached on the peace of the beach.

The sun had sunk lower in the sky by the time she collected her towel and slipped her sandals back on. She made her way across the beach and paused to take one last look at the view of sunlight on the water before she turned back toward the resort. She drew in a calm, deep breath that seemed to fill her lungs with tranquility itself. Erica was right; now that she was here, she *never* wanted to leave.

As she spun around, she collided with a wall of hard muscle and stumbled back. She barely stopped herself from falling as strong hands curled around her upper arms and lifted her up to stare into Denver Ramsey's gorgeous hazel eyes.

"My apologies." His voice rumbled low and deliciously deep. It sent her straight into dark, delicious fantasies of him in bed and all the things he could say with that voice that would melt her into a puddle.

He didn't know her, so he didn't recognize her—and for that she was grateful. They had never met before, though she had always been aware of him since the day she'd seen photos of him at his father's funeral. But unless he had stalked her online, he wouldn't, *couldn't* know her face. He would soon, and when he did, the charming smile now on his lips would twist into a hateful sneer. She couldn't judge him for it; he had every right to hate her. Still, she had to try to win his account, for herself and her father.

"No, it was my fault. I'm so sorry," she replied.

"The view this time of day is beautiful, isn't it?" he asked as he released her.

"It's stunning." She glanced back at the water before looking at him again.

She had a moment to observe him without his notice. He wore dark-blue swim trunks and held a mask and a snorkel in his hand. His chest was bare, and his skin was golden from the sun. The masculine perfection of his physique, which had been only hinted at in the *Vanity Fair* pictures, was on full display now.

He wasn't simply handsome. He was a sea god who drowned helpless women in the waves of their desperate desire for him. Blair had never imagined any man could live up to fantasies, but Denver put those fantasies to shame. And in a matter of hours, he was likely going to kill her.

"Will you be staying here at the resort long?" Denver asked her.

"What? Oh, yes, about a week. I hope." She deliberately neglected to introduce herself. "And you?" She already knew the answer, of course, but it was better to pretend she didn't.

"Yes," he lied smoothly, perhaps even better than she did. For a second, she was angry with him, but logically she understood. If he went around telling everyone he was the owner of the resort, then he would be swarmed by people wanting both him and his money.

"Can I escort you somewhere?" he offered.

It was tempting—too tempting—to let herself imagine him doing just that, escorting her back to her little bungalow and what could happen if she let him get her anywhere near a bed.

A blush warmed her face, and desire flushed her body with wave after wave of heat.

"I, uh . . . no, I'll be fine. You look like you're headed for a swim. I wouldn't want to interrupt." Her skin pebbled slightly at the feel of his possessive gaze drinking her in. Her nipples hardened into points, and she knew he could see that.

Clearing his throat, he glanced down at his snorkel mask. "Oh . . . right, swimming." Then he flashed her a dazzling smile that just about erased all rational thoughts for a good couple of seconds. "Perhaps I'll see you later?" He raised a brow in a teasing challenge.

"Perhaps." She couldn't resist smiling a little at him before she walked away. Who knew she liked playing with fire? Because when he saw her later, she knew with dreadful certainty that he wouldn't be happy about her being here, and she would definitely get burned.

Denver watched the bombshell in the red bikini saunter away and felt as though his entire body was on fire.

God, he wanted to grab her hips and feel them sway in his hold. She had some serious curves, the kind that made a man forget his name. Speaking of names, he needed to know hers.

She continued down the path to the Siren bungalow. He would have to call Simon and ask who she was. As much as he enjoyed a swim, he now had a far more intriguing prospect in front of him. He pulled his cell out of his pocket and dialed his operations manager.

"Simon, what's my schedule this evening?"

"You have an appointment with an advertising firm. That's at eight p.m."

"Then reserve my table for dinner at seven and send an

invitation to the Siren bungalow. I just met the occupant, and she was something."

Simon chuckled. "Very well. I can do that."

"Who am I meeting with this evening?"

"Let me see . . ." Denver heard a shuffling of paper, and then Simon replied, "The Bay Breeze agency?"

The feeling of elation and excitement for tonight's dinner with the mystery brunette died. "You're sure?"

"Yes. Why, is that a problem?"

Denver trusted Simon like a brother, but he hadn't told him the full story about his father and who had been involved in his downfall. The company that had destroyed Denver's life and his mother's life had a shiny new name, but it was still run by Randall Ashworth—one of the two men who'd wrecked his father. Shock and rage tore through Denver like a riptide.

"I can cancel the meeting. Ms. Ashworth is staying for the week at the resort, but she may leave if I cancel."

A strange ringing filled Denver's ears. "Blair Ashworth is here? On my property?"

"Yes, let's see. Oh . . ." The single syllable held a heaviness that Denver didn't like.

"What is it?" He was certain he wasn't going to like what his friend told him next.

"That woman you thought was something? In the Siren bungalow? That's Blair Ashworth."

"Oh, she's *something* all right," Denver nearly snarled into the phone before he regained control.

"So cancel dinner and the meeting?" Simon queried, concern clear in the softness of his words.

Denver glared at the waves rolling in. Damn the sea and its ability to calm him down when he wanted to rightfully rage.

"No." He gave himself a moment to think. "Go ahead and keep the meeting and send the dinner invite as planned."

"Are you sure?"

"Just do it." Denver hung up.

Maybe he needed that swim after all. Because tonight, he was going to get a close-up view of the daughter of the man who had ruined his life, and then, when he was ready, he would send her running for the hills.

Blair got out of the shower just in time to hear someone knock on the front door of the bungalow. She hastily pulled on a robe and rushed to the front room to open the door. Erica stood there with a dark-blue envelope in her hand.

"What's this?"

"A dinner invitation." She beamed at Blair. "Apparently, my boss ran into you earlier, and he likes you."

"Your boss?" Blair tried to pretend she didn't know who Erica worked for.

"Yeah. He would like you to join him for dinner tonight. If you want to go, the details are in here." She passed Blair the envelope. For a second, Blair almost giggled. It was like she was in middle school again, receiving notes from a boy who liked her.

"Thanks." She watched Erica walk away before she closed the door and opened the envelope.

Miss Siren Bungalow Guest,

I hope you don't mind the forward gesture, but I retained a private table for dinner tonight at seven and would love for you to join me this evening.

Cordially,

The man who rudely bumped into you this afternoon

Blair's heart leapt, then stilled. Denver had invited her to dinner. He didn't know who she was yet, but he would the second she had to tell him her full name.

She desperately wanted to have dinner with him, to see him relaxed and charming. It might give her a chance to charm him outside of a business environment so he'd be in a good mood and willing to listen to her ideas. She'd never get another chance to spend time with him like this if she didn't seize the opportunity. But what could she say? Could she keep her true identity from him during dinner long enough to enjoy herself? If she was smart, she would leave now. Check out and catch a flight home as soon as possible. If she could pitch her campaign to him at least once, she could survive whatever came next, no matter how bad it was.

Blair set the invitation on the dining table and went to dry her hair and dress for dinner. This might be her only night here if he decided to throw her off the property, so she might as well try to enjoy it. She'd figure out a way to keep her name from him somehow, at least long enough to have dinner.

She wore a navy knee-length dress with sleeves and a pair of blue heels that were less beachy and more formal since she would be going to his office right after dinner. Even if he did toss her out, at least she would look nice. She tried to enjoy the walk to the lobby, even though she felt a bit like she was walking to her doom. The sun setting below the main building and the golden chandeliers above illuminated the entrance of the lobby and the interior. The blue, gold, and silver walls seemed almost to ripple with the light as though the lobby was underwater.

"Are you here for dinner?" a man in a hotel uniform asked her.

"Yes. I received this." She held up the invitation.

When the man saw it, his eyes lit up. "Right this way. Your table is ready."

She was escorted through the main dining room. The back wall was a massive aquarium with a full coral reef filled with tropical fish. It was a detailed habitat that rivaled any of the best aquariums in the United States. The floor-to-ceiling glass let the dinner guests view the underwater world in all its stunning glory. Suddenly her lips parted in shock at what she saw.

"First time?" The man escorting her to her table smiled and nodded at what had captured her attention.

A man and a woman were swimming in the tank. No . . . a merman and a mermaid. Their blue-and-green tails shimmered in the light as they drifted past a part of the reef. It was an utterly breathtaking thing to witness.

"Those aren't . . . ?" She laughed nervously, wondering if she was imagining it.

"Real?" He laughed. "No, but they are wearing the most expensive, most realistic silicone tails available. Mr. Ramsey wants guests to have a magical experience while they're here."

It was definitely magical. And it completely changed her initial vision for the ad campaign she had planned to pitch him.

"Here at the Seven Seas, we want you to feel like you're part of the ocean," the hotel employee added as she followed him around the back side of the aquarium. They passed by dozens of candlelit tables with couples dining in the dim gold light. The faint clink of silverware on expensive china and the distant roar of the sea was a lulling combination.

As they rounded the side of the aquarium, she entered

a private area with a single circular booth that faced the tank from the opposite side of the dining hall. Of course, the owner of a hotel would have a discreet place to dine with his guests or alone.

Blair halted as she saw a tall figure in a suit standing silhouetted in front of the glass of the aquarium.

"Here we are," the employee announced before abandoning her.

The tall figure turned around. She had known it would be Denver, but seeing him in person, with a glowing underwater world of magic and color behind him, was something she would never forget as long as she lived.

"I'm glad you came," he said, a teasing smile on his lips. "I was afraid you might not."

"I almost didn't . . ." That wasn't a lie, at least.

"I'm Denver," he said and held out a hand to her.

"Blair." She smiled back, glad she didn't have to say her last name. He held her hand a moment too long, while an electric shock of pure feminine awareness rippled through her. Now more than ever, she wished their fathers didn't have a dark history, that she and Denver really were just two strangers who had bumped into each other on the most gorgeous beach she had ever seen and were now about to have a romantic dinner together.

"Please, sit." He waved for her to slide into the booth. Then he joined her on the other side.

"So, according to the person who delivered the dinner invitation, you own the hotel," she said, still playing the game of not knowing who he was and hating herself for it.

"I do." He was studying her, his gaze intense, as though if he looked at her long enough he would be able to read her every thought. "Let's not talk about mundane things, like what we do for a living. I want to know you. What makes you *you*?"

Blair hadn't expected that. He was purposely keeping her off guard, and she didn't know why. If he knew who she really was, he'd be shouting at her—or calling for security.

"Like . . . like what?" She reached for her cloth napkin on the table, absently twisting the fabric in her lap. When she noticed him looking, she put one hand on the table, trying to straighten her silverware.

He reached across the table and caught her hand in one of his, holding it still.

"You're nervous," he observed.

"Yes, of course I am." She tried to laugh.

"Is it because of me?" He stroked his thumb over her hand, and again, sparks seemed to leap between them. "Are you afraid of me? Afraid I'll ravish you right here on the table, Miss Ashworth?"

Her gaze shot to his in sudden panic as he said her name.

"Yes." His lip curled in a cold half smile. "I know who

you are. I also know that you secured a meeting with me through my operations manager for later this evening." Denver's eyes never left hers as the teasing warmth from moments ago completely vanished.

Blair started to slide away, but his grip tightened on her wrist. He wasn't hurting her, but she couldn't get free.

"Stay, Miss Ashworth. This is what you came for, isn't it? I must say I'm impressed that you had the courage to set foot on my island."

Blair bit back the retort that he didn't own the Bahamas, but she kept quiet because she wanted to try to last long enough to pitch her campaign to him.

When she forced herself to relax, he let go of her hand and leaned back with a smug expression that should not have turned her on, but God help her it did. She couldn't help but hate him for hating her and how that turned her on. She was going to need therapy, thanks to him, because if he tried to ravish her on the table like he said, she'd not only let him—she'd be begging for it. This was not a side of herself she was familiar with. She'd always enjoyed sex, had a healthy appetite for it, but she'd never wanted someone as bad as she wanted this man, and it made zero sense. It was like a rabbit wanting to cuddle up beside a wolf.

"If you know why I'm here, then why are you letting me stay? Why haven't you tossed me out?"

"That's just it—I *don't* know why you're here." A

flash of puzzlement appeared in his eyes as he continued to study her.

"I'm here to pitch an advertising campaign to you."

He laughed, the sound both harsh and beautiful all at once.

"There's more to it than that. I want the whole story. You tell me—and be honest about it!—and I'll let you make your pitch before I send you packing."

Blair held her tongue. She couldn't tell him the full truth; it was too personal, and he would think she was hoping her dad would get back into the company he had been forced out of. None of that would help her cause. So the only option was to keep it simple.

"I'm trying to earn a promotion. Right now I'm just an art development director, but if you become a client for five years, then I'll be promoted to an account executive. It's been my dream for a long time."

"That's it? A simple promotion? Miss Ashworth—" He scoffed.

A flash of anger made her interrupt him. She wasn't going to let him push her around. "It's *not* simple. My boss is an egotistical jerk who will never promote me unless I do the impossible . . ."

"Like win over someone impossible . . . like *me*." Comprehension lit his eyes, and then pity slipped over his features for a second before he masked it.

She didn't want his pity. "I told you the reason. Now

will you still hear me out and let me pitch you?" She didn't dare mention anything about regaining control of her father's half of the company. That would be the last thing to win him over as an ally.

Denver leaned in, a crooked smile curving his lips as he spoke. "Miss Ashworth, I'll be blunt. There's only *one* thing I want from you, and I'm quite sure it's the last thing you would agree to." His voice was deep, full of wry amusement, and it rattled the battlements of her defenses, threatening to reach the very core of her. How could a man like him be so damn hot when he was insulting her? The lust burning in his hazel eyes scorched her.

"If you think I'll sleep with you to get your business, you're not as brilliant as I thought." She paused, reined in her temper, and regained her control. The heat, both of desire and anger, still simmered between them, but she forced herself back on track. She licked her lips, and his eyes tracked the movement and she swallowed. Blair straightened her shoulders and projected more confidence than she actually felt. "*Please*, just let me pitch to you. Half an hour, then you never have to see me again."

He didn't take his eyes off her. "Very well, you have the floor." He gestured like a king, giving his royal permission to begin her plea.

Shit . . . She wasn't ready, not after having seen the place up close. There were so many things that she wanted to include in her pitch. She felt now that her presentation was utterly inadequate. But this was her one chance to get through to him. Blair cleared her throat and leaned forward, letting herself fall into work mode.

"Well, now that I'm here, there are things I want to add to my presentation. Your current marketing strategy is missing some key points. What I've seen here makes Seven Seas magical. But that glow is missing from your current materials. Right now, online at least, this feels just like another high-end resort, of which there are hundreds."

"*Ouch*," Denver replied with a dark smirk at her bluntness.

"You wanted honesty." She let that statement fill the air between them.

His answer was a slight nod of acknowledgment, his eyes heavy on her face.

She continued, more confident now. "This place is incredible. Truly. You have taken it to another level. It's not just expensive aquariums and cabanas by the beach. It's the dedication to details, and it's a focus on the magic of the sea in an alluring and mysterious Atlantis sort of way rather than a Disneyland approach. Not that Disney is bad, but you have a different clientele, and we need not only to sell them on this place, but we also need to captivate them with the magic you bring to the resort."

She faltered as she realized the various meanings he could take from that. Her eyes widened and her breath stopped, and he watched her, the aquarium light dancing on his strong jaw. She buried the sudden swell of a dozen confusing emotions within her. She had to finish her comments strong while she had his full attention.

"That needs to be essential in your branding, and it's missing right now. If you ever want to expand this to a new location and need new investment partners, you'll have to solidify your brand."

Blair stopped talking as she realized she had gone into strategizing mode in front of a man who seemed torn between strangling her and fucking her brains out. He didn't say anything for a long second. She tried to ignore the heat the man was giving off, and the way her senses picked up on everything. Her own skin felt hot, and a faint sheen of sweat emerged on her face, but she didn't move. She didn't say anything else, even though she was desperate to plead with him to give her a fair shot. Just being near him had awoken something fierce inside her that wasn't simply physical attraction; she felt challenged to prove to him that she was skilled and every bit his equal if they worked together on this campaign.

"I will give you two days to do whatever you want on my island and add whatever you need to your pitch." He leveled a dark, serious look at her that made her entire body burst into invisible flames. "*Two days*, Miss Ashworth."

He got out of the booth and strode away, leaving her completely alone. The light from the massive aquarium rippled across the dark-blue leather of the booth and the table and onto her hands. They were trembling.

She was still alive. She was still here, and she had bought herself a few days' time to try to win him over. Had she really gotten through to him? Maybe a little. She shivered as she recalled the look in his eyes a second before he stood. It was a look of raw lust. He had only one thing on his mind, and it *wasn't* her presentation. He had warned her; all he wanted was her in his bed. While the most basic animal part of her wanted that too, it would be the worst idea she'd ever had.

Focus on the project. Not the insanely gorgeous sea god who probably would give you the best hate sex of your life. Yeah. Definitely don't think about that.

If you'd like to know what happens next, get the book HERE!

About the Author

Lauren Smith is an Oklahoma attorney by day, author by night who pens adventurous and edgy romance stories by the light of her smart phone flashlight app. She knew she was destined to be a romance writer when she attempted to re-write the entire *Titanic* movie just to save Jack from drowning. Connecting with readers by writing emotionally moving, realistic and sexy romances no matter what time period is her passion. She's won multiple awards in several romance subgenres including: New England Reader's Choice Awards, Greater Detroit BookSeller's Best Awards, and a Semi-Finalist award for the Mary Wollstonecraft Shelley Award.

To connect with Lauren, visit her at:
www.laurensmithbooks.com
lauren@Laurensmithbooks.com